Ranger's End Game

Northern States Pack #1

By Lee Oliver

Ranger's End Game (Northern States Pack #1)

Copyright © Lee Oliver, 2017

ALL RIGHTS RESERVED

Cover Design by Lee Oliver

Model – ABA_046 Courtesy of Paul Henry Serres Photographer (Exclusive license) Copyright Paul Henry Serres.

White wolf and background - Elena Schweitzer | Dreamstime.com

First Edition February 2017

Ranger's End Game is a work of fiction. Names, characters, places and incidents are either the

Table of Contents

Note from the Author

Hello and thank you for taking a chance in reading the first Northern States Pack book. These will be a series of short stories of between 50 – 100 pages. As with all my stories, they feature paranormal men falling in love with other men. I am a huge fan of the true mate trope as these stories will show. I am also hoping to write other shorts as they spring to mind unrelated to this series just because I can – I get a lot of crazy ideas ☺.

These stories are all standalone. Some of them, like this one, include an epilogue which does introduce you to the character in the next book, but you don't have to read this as a series. Every story and couple will be different and there are no long ranging story arcs in these books.

Some of you may know me as Lisa Oliver, author of the Cloverleah Pack, the Bound and Bonded series, the Alpha and Omega series, Stockton Wolves, and the Balance series featuring angels and demons. If you are a fan of longer books, I encourage you to give them a try. All my books are M/M (or M/M/M), guarantee an HEA and with absolutely no cheating.

Hug the One you love,

Lee/Lisa.

Dedication

To my good friends, Judy and Phil who don't care what name I write under and who support me every day. Thank you.

Chapter One

Ranger stood with his arms akimbo and glared at the twenty odd men clustered around the stage. Young, wannabe alphas, most of whom carried an air of entitlement that came from youth and position. *This is going to be a pain in the ass,* he thought as everyone eyed him expectantly. The urge to knock a few sneers off faces grew by the second.

"You'll soon knock the asshole out of them," Cam, his second in command muttered. "Where the hell did this lot come from?"

"Council orders," Ranger whispered conscious of sharp ears. "Developing pack unity is the official position."

"You don't think that's true." Cam knew him too well.

"Doesn't really matter what I think," Ranger replied watching some of the bigger men start to show signs of restlessness. They'd be the first ones to cause trouble. "Meet me at the Swamp later on."

"Ready to kick alpha butt?"

"Someone has too," Ranger said shortly, although why he was being punished with this inane assignment was anyone's guess. He sure as hell didn't know and that bugged him almost as much as the men waiting for him.

"Listen up," Ranger didn't bother raising his voice. One advantage of issuing orders to shifters is they all have excellent hearing. "I'm sure you received your welcome packets from the Council full of the normal blather about how you're here to fulfill your destiny as one of the Council's new elite fighting force."

"Yeah," A larger, bullish man standing at the front had the balls to meet Ranger's eyes although he didn't hold them long. "But all we've been doing is standing around watching you two gabbing like you've nothing better to do. When my dad called the council last week, I was assured of a private room, an omega to tend to my needs and I'm hungry. So if you've got something to say, get on with it. I haven't got all day."

Ranger didn't hesitate. He didn't even leave the stage; he simply took two steps forward, reaching and grabbing the man by his thick neck and lifting him off the ground.

"You've been conscripted, pup," Ranger growled. "You signed the forms. For the next week, your ass is mine and if you think for one second anyone is going to wash your clothes, serve your food or warm your bed at night you're in for a rude awakening."

"My father is the Alpha of one of the largest packs in the West. You can't treat me like this," The man didn't look as cocky anymore. It was probably the first time he'd been manhandled in his life.

"Wrong!" Ranger found the spot he was looking for and pressing hard for just two seconds, dropped the whining heap on the ground. "Anyone else want a go?" he said straightening up and running a hand through his long black hair. "Might as well get the bullshit out of the way first."

There was muttering among the men but it quickly stopped as Ranger's eyes swept the crowd. "You can call me Ranger," he continued when everyone settled down. "This is Cam, my second-in-command. Over the next seven days, you will rise at five and work until I tell you to stop. You can forget anything you thought you knew about fighting or protecting yourself and others. You're in a totally different ballgame now."

At least the men were listening to him. "I don't care what your pack position is; who your father plays poker with or how many friends you think you have on the council. If you don't do as you're told immediately, you are out of the program. If you don't keep up; you're out. You cause problems for anyone, no matter who they are or for whatever reason; you're out." Ranger surveyed the group. The muttering at the back was getting louder and he snarled.

"Anyone who doesn't think they're capable of following orders, the gate is that way." He pointed to his left. "It's a twenty-mile hike to town and I suggest you don't try making the trip at night."

"We're wolves, sir, we can see in the dark." At least the young man speaking had a certain level of respect in his tone. Ranger found he liked the word sir falling from the boy's lips.

"You may be able to see, but the land mines are buried and scent-free. As soon as darkness falls the woods surrounding this compound are protected by motion sensors. You'll have those balls of yours blown off before you get twenty feet from the gate. Guaranteed." The young man had a fetching blush that highlighted his blond features and fair skin.

"Training starts at 0500," Ranger said, wrenching his gaze from the young man. "Cam will direct you to the mess hall and then to your dorm rooms. Anyone not in the quad by 0500 will be…." he cupped his ear and raised an eyebrow.

"OUT Ranger." Maybe there was hope for the youngsters yet.

*****

Aiden Chalmers didn't consider himself a small man, but faced with the men he was meant to be training with for the next week, not to mention the enigmatic Ranger and his cheery-as-a-wet-week second, he was feeling at a decided disadvantage. Growing up the youngest of six brothers, Aiden relied on skill, cunning and when that didn't work, pure speed to keep him out of trouble. The churning in his gut made him realize none of those things were going to help him in the coming week.

"That big guy thinks he's better than us," A redheaded bear grumbled beside him. Aiden shrugged. He was keeping his opinion of Ranger to himself. When Ranger lifted arrogant-Al off his feet without breaking a sweat, Aiden had a lot of trouble hiding his arousal. With wolves being able to smell sex in the air, he was glad he'd worn a splash of cologne. Not something he usually did, but he was grateful for the foresight.

"Will Al be all right?" Aiden asked instead.

"Don't care," the redhead growled. "He's another one who thinks his shit doesn't stink. It was a dumb ass thing calling out the boss like that in front of everyone else. Nah, the only way to bring that man down is to show a bit of stealth. Get him on his own." The redhead's grin was malicious and Aiden felt a shiver of alarm run down his spine. He was pleased to see they'd arrived at the mess hall.

14

"Bags along the wall," Cam yelled. "Trays, food, tables. You have fifteen minutes. Move it."

"What the fuck?" The redhead grumbled.

Aiden looked across at the food counters and his stomach growled. Another problem of growing up with so many older siblings is that you had to eat fast or your food ended up on someone else's plate. The food counters were full of meats, vegetables and Aiden caught the whiff of properly made gravy. Food, glorious food. He wasn't complaining. He grabbed a plate and started filling it.

"What's wrong?" The redhead was still complaining. By the time he sat down, the redhead knocking his elbows, he wished he'd kept his mouth shut. The redhead, who still hadn't bothered to introduce himself, complained about the texture of the steak, the stringiness of the beans, and the lack of cream and butter in the potatoes. His rant on why grown men shouldn't be deprived of beer or spirits with a meal was still in mid-flow when a loud bell sounded.

"Scraps in the garbage can, plates on the tray, get your bags and line up by the door," Cam said loudly. "You have one minute. Move it!" he yelled when no one seemed inclined to move.

"I haven't finished my dinner." The redhead complained as he got slowly to his feet. *Maybe if you'd used your mouth for chewing instead of complaining you'd be finished*, Aiden thought but he didn't see the point in saying anything out loud. "Get through the one-week training and I'll release your trust fund," his father told him. That was Aiden's major goal. Aligning himself with troublemakers and whiners wasn't going to help him reach that objective. Using the milling around of the men as they grabbed their bags as an excuse to ditch his redheaded companion, Aiden was determined to stick to himself, keep his head down and hopefully stay alive. *Just seven days and I'm free;* he almost smiled at the thought.

*****

"So, what's your verdict? Can we do anything with them?" Ranger growled as Cam slid into the booth across from him. Cam grimaced as he swigged the bottle Ranger had ready for him.

"I don't know how any of them got through boot camp," Cam said dismissively. "Standards have definitely dropped since our day."

"They didn't come from boot camp," Ranger took a pack of cigarettes from his shirt pocket and offered one to Cam before lighting one himself.

"What the fuck?" Cam's eyebrows rose. "They had to have had some training. Military? Police? Some special enforcer school I've never heard of?"

"All fresh off the farm," Ranger blew out a long stream of smoke watching it lazily spin in the air. The Swamp was one of the few places on the council's not-so-secret base he could smoke and not worry about being challenged. Anyone who came into the dingy bar did so to drink, relax and kept to themselves.

There were a few men scattered around the room. Some Ranger knew by sight; others he didn't. But none of them concerned him. He might not know them, but they would know of him. The long blue streak in his hair and the tattooed star under his left eye marked him as the best assassin the council had on its books and Ranger spent a lifetime building a reputation of being a kill first, ask questions later type of guy.

"We've been demoted?"

Ranger looked back at Cam and shook his head.

Cam leaned across the table. "Did you piss off one of the eggheads again?"

Ranger's lips twitched around his smoke as he shook his head again. His friend had no respect for council members. "Not to my knowledge."

"Then how did the council's deadliest assassin and his faithful sidekick end up babysitting a bunch of kids?"

"If you hadn't spent the last month shagging your way through the eastern states, you'd know." Cam was one of the few men Ranger relaxed around enough to tease. They were the same age, raised in the same pack and when the council called they trained together. Quickly rising through the ranks, Ranger was known as a hands-on killer, while Cam provided backup, researched their targets and could take out an eye from three hundred feet with the large Bowie knife he kept strapped to his thigh.

Cam grinned, sinking back in his chair and raising his bottle in salute. "You're not the only one with a reputation to maintain. I just have my dance partners gasping for different reasons than yours. So, what's going on? Why the fuck are we here?"

Ranger looked around; no one was paying them any attention but he leaned over the table anyway. "The official version is that our illustrious bosses decided to create a task force designed to breach pack barriers and take care of territory disputes, rogue shifters, and inter-species issues. All packs were sent an order, invitation, call it what you like, to send one man for training purposes."

"I bet that upset some alpha females in the packs."

Raising an eyebrow, Ranger snorted. "We all know how advanced in thinking the council is. They were very specific. The men had to be between twenty-four and twenty-nine years old, alpha born but not in line to lead their pack."

"The spares in other words," Cam shook his head. "No wonder these guys have attitude. What happens after a week? With no previous training, these guys aren't going to be fit for field work."

"I don't know," and that's what pissed Ranger off the most. He hated feeling like a mushroom. "Dominic called me personally. Told me my vacation was cut short effective immediately and that I had to get my ass back here to spend a week training these guys 'to the best of my ability.' When I got here, I got handed the same welcome pack of bullshit sent to the packs, and told to make full use of the base facilities."

"There're a ton of other guys better suited to this job," Cam's eyes narrowed. "Any of the council enforcers or one of the captains of the guards would be more qualified. Why you?"

"Exactly," Ranger sat back and grabbed his bottle, emptying it. Cam was thinking things over; it's what he did best. Whereas Ranger was action-orientated, Cam made the perfect partner. He thought things through; examined them from every angle and took his time making any decision. Ranger watched his blond, blue-eyed friend, happy to wait.

Cam was slightly smaller than he was in height and build, but in every other way, they were polar opposites. Cam was fair, Ranger sported a deep tan. Cam's sexual exploits were a well-known fact; he'd fuck anyone regardless of gender, species or position. Ranger spent his downtime on his own. Having sex meant getting close to people and he couldn't be bothered. When his urges got too much, a quick visit to a club usually resulted in someone face-planted against an alley wall so he could get his rocks off. A hand to rub off on was all he offered in exchange. Ranger made no apologies for who he was or how he acted; Cam was Mr. Smooth all the way.

"This training," Cam said quietly. "Were there any specifics? Are they to work as a team, or are we finding out their individual skills and honing them?"

Ranger shook his head. "They think they're working as a team. I've been told to make reports on them individually, outlining any 'outstanding or unusual skills.'"

"That means you're going to have to work with all of them one-on-one at some point."

"So I've been told," Ranger quirked an eyebrow. "Are you thinking what I'm thinking?"

"The eggheads are after your ass," Cam shook his head. "The sleazy shits. They spent twenty years training you and now that no one can take you out, they think one of these toy soldiers can do it?"

"It wouldn't be the first time they've tried. Why else would they be using the spares?" Ranger frowned. "I don't like this. I don't like this shit at all. I read the fine print on the agreement signed by these inductees. No return; no retribution. Every pack alpha signed it."

"So if anyone tries to take you out, and you as alpha assassin kill them...."

"I'll have an angry pack alpha on my ass while the council sits there completely absolved from responsibility."

"Best make sure you don't kill anyone then," Cam offered a grin. "It's only for a week."

"It's going to be a long fucking week."

Chapter Two

Gods, it's going to be a long week, Aiden thought as he pulled himself up the rope ladder and grabbed the handle for the flying fox. Breakfast was hearty but hours ago and he still had another mile of the "training course" as Ranger euphemistically put it when he sent them on their way, before lunch. "More like torture course," he muttered as he rubbed his hands on his jeans. The man who went before him was sweaty. Getting a firmer grip, Aiden jumped and pushed over the mud, landing safely on the other side.

Redhead, turns out his name was Brian, wasn't so lucky. He was face-planted in the mud as Aiden sailed over him; Cam yelling at him to get up. There was no sign of Ranger. That was a man born to lead the pack. He'd sprinted off in front of everyone, showing them how it was done. Aiden tried to keep pace, and while he had the speed, the obstacles were a different matter. His arms ached in their sockets, his pants were ripped and his elbows and knees were grazed.

"Keep going," Cam yelled and Aiden pushed himself forward. "Last one back does the dishes."

Oh hell no, I'm not going to be last. Aiden ran another twenty yards, dropped to the ground with a groan and winced as he put his knees and elbows to work. He hated the crawling parts of the course more than anything else. But his slim build worked well for him during this part of the workout. He heard another trainee, Gerald swear as the epaulets on the fancy shirt he wore got caught on the ropes; another man with a temper as big as his shoulder width and ridiculous fashion sense. Aiden was glad he'd opted for comfortable jeans and a muscle shirt.

Breaking free of the ropes, Aiden staggered to his feet and groaned under his breath as he saw the ten-foot wall coming up. Spring up. Get steady on the top and then jump down on the other side. Not a problem for a shifter. But Aiden's eyes narrowed as he saw Al sitting up on the wall and his friend Dan standing to one side of it. Al spent last night moaning about assassin high-handedness and how he could 'take the guy.' Personally, Aiden didn't think that was possible. He'd used his time researching the hunky looking man with the star tattoo. Ranger was a living, breathing, walking legend. *And totally dreamy, not that I need to be thinking about that right now.*

He took a quick look over his shoulder. Cam was still urging Brian and a couple of the others to move their lazy asses. But they hadn't made it to the net yet. There was no one in front. Gritting his teeth Aiden ran for the wall and jumped. Shit. His hands were too small to get a grip and he fell back; Al and Dan laughing their heads off.

Picking himself up, Aiden ignored his so-called teammates and ran and jumped again. This time he got a hold on the far edge of the ledge and he kicked against the wall, trying to get leverage. He was just about to swing his leg over when a strong grip on his wrist stopped him.

"What ya going to give me, if I give you a hand up?" Al leered.

"I'm fine, I can do it myself." Aiden tried to get back on the ground, but Al was strong. He was left dangling and his wrist would be bruised. "Let me go. You heard Ranger. Everyone has to complete the trial on their own." He tried looking back. Brian was stuck under the rope mat and Cam was losing his temper with him. No help there. He couldn't see in front of him because he was stuck on the damn wall."

"Why listen to Ranger's crap?" Al snarled. "He's not your alpha."

"Neither are you; let me GO!" Aiden struggled, pushing against the wall, bracing his feet under him so he'd have more pulling power. Al tightened his grip but Aiden had been bullied before. He tugged with his arms, pushing against the wall with his feet and with a cry Al toppled off the wall, Aiden crushed beneath him.

"Why you little snot."

Aiden barely had time to blink and Al's fist crashed into his stomach; then his face; then his ribs. There was no way he could fight someone fifty pounds heavier and squashing him. Calling on his wolf, he snarled his way through the change; snapping at Al as soon as his snout and teeth appeared.

*****

"I knew you were going to be a fucking troublemaker," Ranger muttered as he sprinted around the wall. Al and Dan had the wolf caged against it. The wolf was showing an impressive set of teeth but wasn't attacking. Which he had every right to do. Ranger wondered what had happened to Al and his crony when they took longer to complete the course than they should have. He'd doubled back, seeing those buttheads causing problems on the last obstacle. He was just about to step in and stop them when it was the pretty blond's turn. Ranger forced himself to hold back, waiting to see just how bad Al would get. He'd heard the blond's determination to finish the course by himself, and the leer behind Al's offer. Ranger hated bullies and sexual predators were road kill as far as he was concerned.

Deciding words were a waste of breath, Ranger latched onto Dan who was closest and turned him, slamming his face straight into the wall beside the wolf. Dan's nose made a satisfying crunch and the man fell to his knees whimpering. Al immediately went on the offensive but Ranger was faster, blocking blow after blow, barely breaking a sweat.

Al on the other hand; Ranger had met his type a hundred times before. Using brawn, not brains, counting on his body weight behind a punch to do the damage. Of course, the punches had to land first and Al wasn't having any luck with that. Ranger kept countering until Al's face was bright red and dripping with sweat; then one perfectly executed leg sweep behind the knees and the big man went down with a thud.

Ignoring the men on the ground, Ranger stepped over to check the wolf whose lips were still curled in a snarl. "You going to take me on?" he said with a smile. The wolf shook his head. "Let me check you over and then you shift."

He ran his hands over the wolf's fur, checking ribs and stomach, shoulder and hip bones. The wolf turned away at first, but then…shit, the realization must have hit him the same time as his scent hit

Ranger. *Oh crap, this wasn't meant to happen to me.* The wolf had no such reservations. Ranger found himself toppled with a lap full of wolf; the creature happily rubbing Ranger's face, chest and anywhere else he could reach.

"Not here," he warned in the wolf's ear and the wolf immediately stopped. With a low whine, he backed off but didn't go far.

A beefy hand appeared over his shoulder. "Need a hand up?" Cam finally arrived, a mud-splattered, chest-heaving Brian behind him. Ranger took the hand, and hard as it was, he ignored the wolf in favor of the two men on the ground.

"I see how it is," Al sneered. "Got your favorites picked out already. No doubts how he's gonna pass. Puny body, no fighting power, but I bet he sucks like a Hoover."

Ranger clenched his fists. Being powerful didn't mean that power should be used, although his control was becoming an issue. He could cheerfully gut both bullies and not lose any sleep. "There were only three rules I outlined yesterday. Not complicated, yet you broke two of them. What were they?"

"Follow orders and don't cause trouble with anyone for anything," Cam said helpfully.

"And you went for the double." It was Ranger's turn to sneer. "Don't bother trying to defend yourself. This whole course is monitored electronically and even if it wasn't, I've been watching you two for plenty long enough. You've got fifteen minutes to collect your stuff and clear the base. You should cover twenty miles by nightfall."

"I'll call my dad and get him to send someone to collect me at the gate," Al said, struggling to his feet. "I never wanted to be in this program anyway. I don't know why Dad sent me."

"Personal phones don't work within a five-mile radius of the base,"

Ranger pulled out his phone and clicked a couple of screens. "And as of now, your internet access is revoked. I suggest you start walking unless you want to find yourself in lockup."

"You can't do that, it's a violation of our rights," Al was not a happy camper and Ranger decided to make things worse.

"Your dad signed away your rights when he signed the forms that got you in here. And before you go whinging to Daddy, I suggest you think long and hard *why* he'd send you here. He agreed to the no return; no restitution clause the same as everyone else. Can you think of any reason why your dad wants you dead? Because anyone with an ounce of sense knows the death rate in council training is approximately fifty percent."

Al's face went white; his mouth flopped about a bit and then he stormed off. It was the wolf's whine that attracted Ranger's attention. Shit. Making Al question his family bonds was one thing... "Shift back," Ranger said quietly. "I don't want you at the dorms till those goons are gone. Actually, no," he added seeing the start of the shimmer. "Finish the course on four feet and I'll take you for a shower and medical attention after that."

The wolf tilted his head as if to say, "you kidding me?" But Ranger didn't change his expression. Huffing loudly, the wolf backed away from the wall, took a fast run and jump, clearing it completely and headed for the finish line.

"You and I are having a serious talk when you've finished with the little furball. But you'd better run if you're going to catch him," Cam said slapping Ranger on the shoulder. "Now come on Brian, let's get your fat ass over the wall or we'll miss lunch."

Chapter Three

I've got a mate...my dad wants me dead...I have a mate...my dad... Yep, the thinking wasn't doing Aiden any favors and nor was the enigmatic Ranger. He made the finish line easily enough, and knew with shifting, the grazes on his knees and elbows would be gone too, along with most of the bruising he hoped. But to know that, he'd have to shift. Ranger told him to stay in wolf form and wait for him in a small room by his office. It seemed one of the council members had come to visit and wasn't happy with the way Ranger was running things. Aiden edged closer to the door to hear more.

"These men need hand-to-hand, one-on-one training; you're supposed to be teaching them your skills. Assault courses are for the regular soldiers." The councilman's voice was a lot higher in pitch than Ranger's.

"Sir, you gave us a week. With all due respect, nobody can learn my skills in that short of time. I thought you wanted me to see how they worked as a team and assumed the best ones would be picked for further training on completion."

"I've got a hundred soldiers already," the councilman didn't sound happy. "These guys are supposed to be an elite task force. They're not going to get to that point running assault courses."

"They're not going to get to that point in a week, no matter what I put them through. Sir," Aiden wondered if he was the only one who could hear the tinge of anger in Ranger's voice. "The assault course taught us a lot about the caliber of the men, in just one session. Some are good – they have strength and speed and once they stopped whining they showed promise. Others will be lucky if they last a week," Aiden wondered what category he fell into. "We've culled two already – I've sent them off base. This is working. You'll get some good men out of this."

"You didn't kill them? What are you doing sending men off base?"

Aiden was sure he wasn't the only one reeling in shock. Was Ranger expected to kill his teammates? From the sounds of things, Ranger was just as surprised. "Sir, I did see the contract they signed, but there's no way any alpha would've signed it knowing their men could be killed for insubordination or if they didn't pass the tests. We don't do that to our soldiers."

"No, but we do it to our assassins and that's what you're supposed to be training them for."

"None of these men signed up for assassin training."

"No one ever does," It seemed the councilman had a temper too. "There are only four of you in the whole country. Only four who made it through the training. Now

Marcus is mated and insists on taking that simpering idiot with him wherever he goes which makes assigning him to anything difficult; Sean is talking about retiring, and you've been on active duty over twenty years. I haven't been able to get hold of Levi in over a month."

"If you had work that needed doing, why am I stuck training a bunch of losers? You can use my talents better out in the field."

Aiden's hopes shattered. Ranger thought the trainees were losers and what's worse, he was trying to get the councilman to send him out on other jobs. *He doesn't want to be mated.* Refusing to listen to the rest of the discussion, Aiden moved away from the door and shifted. Carefully opening the small window, he climbed out and unconcerned about his nudity, hurried to his dorm. He had a lot of thinking to do.

*****

Fucking hell, I should've kept my trap shut. Ranger wasn't stupid; he'd heard the slide of the window in the room next to his office, although he was glad Dominic hadn't. Now he had to get Dominic out and drag the blond in for a chat. *It would help if I knew his name. Ugh.*

"Look, Dominic," Ranger reverted to first name basis now he knew the blond wasn't listening. "I don't know what your game is. You pulled me off vacation; told me to train these guys for a week for a freaking task force. Now you're telling me you want assassins. Has the council changed the rules? We don't train others for our jobs; it's too risky. Why isn't Tron doing this?" Tron was his old trainer; brutally fast, hellishly strong and took no shit from anyone. A retired assassin, he put Ranger through two years of hell before he'd been sent on his first job.

"Everyone in existence knows Tron is the assassin trainer," Dominic snapped. "The trainees would be out of here in a flash if he turned up."

"They know I'm an assassin too," Ranger pointed to the star on his face. "Maybe this is the reason no one is signing up for the job. You insist on marking us for the rest of our lives making us pariahs in normal society."

"But they also know current assassins don't train the new guys."

"So, what's your plan? I train these guys for a week, point you in the direction of the ones who'll be useful to you, and then what?"

"They get thrown at Tron and as for the others; well it will depend on what state they're in by the end of the week." Dominic's voice hardened. Ranger felt a cold chill run down his spine.

"Assassin's need a certain frame of mind; an attitude that's pretty rare among shifters. You can't just throw anyone into training with someone like Tron without warning them first."

"It's the law of survival, kill or be killed, which is why I want you to retrieve those two men you kicked out of here earlier."

No way in hell. "They don't have the right attitude. They're bullies and sexual predators. If you bring them back, then you can kiss the effectiveness of this training goodbye."

"They can help get rid of the defective ones; the ones that won't fight back." *Has Dominic always been this callous?*

"I won't train those two. I don't care what you say or do; bring in Marcus or Sean, but I'm warning you; if they come back, I walk."

"You're under orders." Dominic stepped into his personal space and Ranger's wolf growled.

"I work under council orders, and the last order I got from them was a three-month vacation because I hadn't had one in two years; a vacation you interrupted." The last thing Ranger would ever be was scared of Dominic. "Do they know about your little plan to trick people into assassin training?"

There. One twitch, right below Dominic's eye. Ranger knew he'd hit the mark. "I'm not your personal hitman, Dominic. I work for the full council. You push me on this and I'll take it to the next meeting. The two men I expelled do not belong in this camp and I won't take them back."

"We need more assassins; rogues are getting out of hand. The council will see I'm right when I tell them about my plan."

"So go and tell them, and leave me out of it. I will train these guys for the week in general fighting skills and give you my report at the end of it. Then I'm finishing my vacation."

"You said you were happy to go back out in the field," Dominic protested as Ranger steered him towards the door.

"I changed my mind. I feel the strong urge to get away from political bullshit." Ranger slammed the door behind Dominic's retreating ass and then thumped it. *Talk to Cam, go after my mate. Shit, I don't even know his name.* His stomach grumbled. *Fuck. And lunch. Maybe I'll find Cam and my mate there.*

Hunting through the application files on his desk, he quickly found the one he was looking for. *Aiden.* Now, at least he had a name for the face. Stuffing the file into his jacket pocket, Ranger strode out of the office and headed for the mess hall. At least that was his intention. A blushing little omega with a pile of papers put paid to that idea.

Chapter Four

Aiden was lucky to find a table by himself. His episode with Al and Dan and the way his wolf reacted to Ranger had him keeping his head down, refusing to make eye contact with anyone. He knew Brian had been there, but there were two other trainees coming up on the scene when he left. With shifter hearing the way it was, chances are everyone knew he'd been bullied and made a fool of himself. He shoveled his food fast, hoping to get five minutes to himself before the afternoon session.

If I survive the afternoon session, he thought, totally oblivious to the delicious stew for once. He couldn't believe what he'd heard in Ranger's office. There was no way he'd ever be considered for assassin training. Hell, he knew he wouldn't make it into the task force. His only plan had been to survive the week and claim his trust fund. A trust fund his father was supposed to have released three months before on his twenty-fifth birthday. The man had been decidedly cagey about it when Aiden pestered him claiming audits, accountancy forms and all sorts of procedures needed to be gone through first.

Was he counting on me never coming back? Aiden knew his father was disappointed in him. He was built well enough for a wolf shifter, but his brothers were titans in comparison. There would never be any talk of him running a pack and while there was no abuse when he came out to his father, it was a close thing. His brothers, Patrick's and Joseph's reactions were bad enough. Not even a shift got rid of the bruising and he'd been laid up in bed for days.

"Did you get checked out at the infirmary?" Cam slid into the seat across from him. Aiden knew from his research, Cam was Ranger's right-hand man and had been for twenty years or more. Maybe he was the reason Ranger didn't want to mate with him.

"I don't need it, thank you," he said, remembering his manners. "A shift took care of the worst of the damage."

"Your wolf half seems to like my assassin friend," Cam grinned. "You know I'm much more approachable if you fancy a fling."

"Yeah, er, no thank you," Aiden said quickly. "I...my wolf hadn't been free for a while. He just got overexcited. I won't let it happen again."

"Ranger didn't seem to mind," Cam said with a wink. "But come on, that's the bell. I've got a short video for you guys to see this afternoon and then I'm going to pair you guys up and see how you do at sparring."

Brilliant, more bruises. Aiden groaned quietly. It was only his first day. If it got much worse he'd be glad of death before the week was out.

*****

Ranger growled as he shoved yet another piece of paper at the hapless assistant who was cowering quietly by his desk. Lunch time was a distant memory. He hadn't had a chance to see Aiden, let alone talk to him. It seemed throwing two men off the base required more paperwork than if he'd killed them. "That'd better be the last of them," he snarled as he saw the young man rifling through more wretched forms.

"Oh…er…yes, Sir. I…er…er…if you need anything else please let me know." The young man's face was scarlet; his pants were tented and Ranger sighed.

"It's Cam you want for that sort of thing," he said, trying to keep the snap out of his voice. "But that reminds me, I'll need forms to register my mating. I assume you have such a thing?"

"Mating sir? Yes sir." At least the young man could run off with a good reason for Ranger's refusal of his blatant offers.

"Just leave it on my desk. I'll fill it in later. In the meantime, can you tell me where the task force group is expected now?" As with any base every group, training session, and fart were recorded somewhere.

The young wolf looked at the clock on the wall. "They were scheduled in the media room directly after lunch. But they were only booked there for thirty minutes. They're due in the gym after that for the rest of the afternoon."

The gym. Hand-to-hand fighting. Ranger remembered Cam suggesting it over breakfast. *Bloody hell, after Al's accusations they'll kill him.*

"If anyone needs me, I'll be at the gym," he yelled as he sprinted out of his office, determined no one was going to stop him a second time.

I'm going to kill him; I've had it up to my fucking ears with this shit. It seemed Brian, actually Aiden didn't think it was Brian who started it, but *someone* decided to mention his little wolf display over Ranger. The comments about his necessity to be on his knees to complete the course had been coming thick and fast all afternoon. It seemed all wolves had the same idea when they looked at him. Aiden was well past flattered and on his way to pure fury.

He was in the ring with Gerald. His fourth fight since lunch. Aiden hated fighting for the sake of it, but of course, this was supposedly training so he had no choice but to jump in. Yeah, the guy was bigger and heavier, but he was slow and telegraphed every move. Aiden might not have beaten his six brothers; they preferred to come at him in pairs. But he could take any one of them singly in a fight. He ducked as a meaty fist came his way and spun around, kicking the man behind the knees.

"Another one down, your match again, Aiden," Cam said cheerfully. "Get some water; Brian and Ruff, you're up next."

"You doing okay?" Cam said quietly as Aiden climbed out of the ring. "Those guys seem to be giving you a hard time. You're winning. I'm impressed, but some of these dudes seem to be out for you personally."

"No worse than at home," Aiden said shortly brushing past the blond reason for Ranger not wanting him. And oh, think of the fucking devil, the man himself was standing by the ice chest. Aiden's first instinct was to walk in the other direction, but every man was going through six fights that afternoon and he still had two to go. Dehydration was not going to help.

Neither was Ranger apparently. The man handed him a chilled

bottle of water, a furrow deep above his eyes and his full mouth turned down. Aiden wanted to grab the bottle and walk away, but his feet wouldn't move. His wolf was in a tizzy of excitement just being in sniffing range. That was typical of his wolf; too damn easy by half. The two men stood side by side in silence as they watched Ruff beat Brian into the mat.

"Next," Cam called. Aiden wasn't next, but he was up just afterward. Guessing his initial thoughts about Ranger not wanting him were spot on, he started moving towards the mat.

"Where do you think you're going?" Ranger asked roughly in a low tone.

Aiden turned, deliberately looking Ranger up and down. Damn his mate was fine. Pushing those thoughts aside he said in his own low voice. "I'm up after this fight. I've won four so far. Not bad for a bruised loser, huh?"

Ranger's eyes widened. "But you're...you're you." Aiden knew what his mate could see; slim build, pretty features. His blond curls didn't help. Shirtless, the bruises he'd got from Dan and Al were still visible, and he'd accumulated a few more since then.

"Yes, I am," he said curtly, "and apparently me isn't good enough for you. Your loss."

He turned and walked away in a hurry, the hurt fueling his anger. He'd never been good enough for his father; his brothers treated him like a joke. And now his mate – the one blessed for him by the Fates. *Another freaking joke,* he thought as he waited his turn.

*****

Ranger was torn; not anything he'd coped with before. He could kill anyone and right now he really wanted to kill the fat bruiser who'd managed to land a punch on Aiden's face. Aiden staggered but didn't fall and Cam, freaking Cam ordered the fight to continue. How could his best friend stand by and let his mate get hurt?

Because you didn't tell him you were mates, numbnuts and now Aiden doesn't think you want him either. Ranger was still trying to work out how his mate got that impression. Okay, he'd called the trainees losers, and he might have mentioned he'd prefer to be on a job than stuck at base. But he was talking to Dominic, not his mate. He sidled up beside Cam, his eyes not leaving the ring.

"The young'un's good," Cam whispered, conscious of other ears. "But his little display over you earlier isn't doing him any favors with the team."

Ranger winced as the man fighting Aiden got in another blow to his ribs. Much more, and Aiden would be too hurt to participate in any of the sexy plans Ranger had running through his head. "He's my true mate," Ranger whispered back, determined to put one thing right. Cam's eyes widened and his mouth formed the perfect 'O'. "And if that jerk lands a one more punch, I'm going to kill the fucker."

"You can't intervene; you'll only make matters worse for him. He's been putting up with shit all afternoon because of you. You didn't even take him to see the medics."

"Dominic wanted to see me. Then I had to do the paperwork for expelling Al and Dan. I got here as soon as I could."

"We'll talk about Dominic later," Cam whispered, "But wait, wait for it. Yes, I knew he'd do it. That boy's got good instincts." Ranger watched in surprise as Aiden flung himself on the ropes and using the added power took his opponent's legs out from under him.

"Your round again, Aiden," Cam yelled out. "Jace get your ass up and out of the ring. People are waiting."

"He cheated, the little cocksucker," Jace yelled as he stumbled to his feet. "No one said you could use the ropes like that."

"A trained fighter will use every weapon in his arsenal and anything he can find to win," Ranger's temper was frayed beyond repair. "However, if you want a go with me, I won't touch the ropes, and if you can take me down, you'll have bragging rights. Me being a top assassin and all. Bet that'd look good to your friends." He hopped up onto the skirt of the ring, stepping over the ropes as if they were nothing.

"You're an assassin," Jace gulped. "You fight to kill."

"And so should you," Ranger made it sound like it was the most natural thing in the world. "This isn't a holiday camp; it's a council training camp with a fifty percent kill rate and that's without having an assassin as your head trainer. Didn't any of you guys do your homework before you signed up?"

From the mutterings in the watching crowd, it seemed none of them did. "You can take that up with your alphas, parents or whoever it was who cosigned your form when this week is over. But let this be a lesson to you. Read the fine print. There's no retribution on me if you don't make it home at the end of the week."

A ripple of shock ran through the trainees and Cam grinned ruefully. "I'm guessing training is over for the day. You heard the boss; go and read your contract, all of it. I'll see you all again at 0500 hours. Unless you thought a night run was in order, Ranger."

"Nope, I have other things to do," Ranger stretched out his arms, knowing it made his muscles ripple. Jace went white. "I'm taking my true mate into town for a private dinner. Coming Aiden?"

Aiden's wasn't the only mouth open in shock as Ranger casually climbed out of the ring, and with a strong arm over his mate's shoulder, escorted him from the gym.

Chapter Five

Roller coasters. I hate roller coasters, and yet that's exactly what Aiden's emotional state was riding on. Up and down, up and down; and now slowly climbing as Ranger confidently drove his black Pontiac down the only road between the nearest town and the base. Ranger hadn't said much at all after his surprise announcement in the gym; simply asking if Aiden had black dress pants and a suitable shirt. He escorted Aiden to his dorm; watched as he rapidly changed clothes, Aiden's face flushing as he did, and then like the perfect gentleman, walked him to the car.

"I need to apologize for what you heard me say to Dominic," Ranger's voice broke the silence. "I wasn't thinking clearly and as soon as I said them, I wanted to take them back. But I was talking to Dominic, not you. I didn't mean to hurt you."

Guessing Dominic was the councilman, Aiden tried to shrug off the memory. It wasn't easy and given Ranger's nose was the sharpest in the shifter world, he answered with the truth. "It hurt a lot and when I didn't see you at lunch, I figured you just didn't want me. I don't blame you," he hastened to add, "I never imagined I was a fit mate for an assassin. I never dreamed of having a mate at all."

"Bit of a shock to me too; but the best one I've ever had," Ranger grinned and as it was the first time Aiden had seen it, he forgave himself for wanting to drool. All he'd seen of Ranger was the stern, unforgiving, and decidedly hunky exterior. That smile lit Ranger's face from the inside and made it glow.

"You didn't have to take me to dinner, you know," Aiden said when he could get his mind back on track. "I would have agreed to the claiming anyway and we both have to be up at five in the morning."

"You deserve better than a quick fuck and bite. I don't think you should continue with the training anyway. You can stay with me until the week is over and then I'll take you back home so you can collect your stuff."

"But I have to finish the training," Aiden said, shocked at Ranger's plan. "If I don't, I don't get my trust fund."

"What?" Ranger roared. The car swerved and he quickly corrected it. Aiden was thrown against the passenger door, and sat up, his hand on his chest. "I'm sorry. I need to pay attention, but you're telling me everything as soon as we get to town."

Aiden sank into silence, unwilling to upset his potential mate any more than he had; although he didn't understand why Ranger reacted so strongly. Surely, Ranger didn't imagine he'd signed up for the task force for the hell of it. He wasn't an idiot.

*****

Must keep calm, must keep calm. Ranger's mantra was doing nothing to control Ranger's rage. He'd barely scanned Aiden's admission form; he just wanted to know his mate's name. But thanks to perfect recall he was now reviewing the document in his mind and the details were making him more indignent by the second. Aiden's signature wasn't evident on the form. It appeared to have been signed by his father. The application shouldn't have been accepted in the first place. Yet it was; suggesting his prospective father-in-law had friends on the council, too.

The rest of the trip went smoothly, at least on the driving side of things. Inside, Ranger could feel cold fury swelling in his gut. He just wasn't sure who to throw it at: Dominic, his future father-in-law or the council drone who rubber-stamped Aiden's application when it didn't carry the man's signature. Parking the car, Ranger huffed out a long breath. "I made reservations," he said, taking Aiden's hand. "There shouldn't be any problems, but if there are, please let me handle them."

Aiden frowned, three little furrows appearing above his eyebrows. "What sort of problems should I be expecting?"

"Not everyone takes kindly to assassins," Ranger tapped the star below his eye. "It's one of the reasons Dominic has so many problems getting people to sign up for training. The tattoo is mandatory."

"I think it looks sexy. Goes well with the streak in your hair," Aiden offered a smile and Ranger melted. It was no wonder Marcus didn't want to work anymore if his mate was as sweet as Aiden. Although Ranger knew Marcus's mate was anything but sweet.

In the restaurant, the hostess did a double take at Ranger's face, but she managed a professional smile. "I have your table ready. Private, as you requested." Ranger nodded his approval and holding tight to Aiden's hand, followed the woman's clip-clopping heels across the floor. He would have loved to seat Aiden by the window; explain a bit more about the town, but his dinner bill would be huge if half the patrons ran out without paying their bill. It was one of the reasons Ranger wasn't a social gadabout.

Their waiter was a young wolf who almost creamed his pants at being within five feet of an assassin. After the menus and orders were sorted, Ranger took Aiden's hand and smiled what he hoped was a friendly smile. "You know, I don't go out much, for obvious reasons, but I wanted to do something nice for you. We didn't get off to a great start. Am I forgiven?"

"You didn't really do anything wrong," Aiden's eyes glowed in the candlelight. "There's nothing to forgive. But thank you."

"I was upset," Ranger chose his words carefully, "upset about your reasons for being in this training course. I notice you didn't sign your application form. You couldn't have known what you were in for and yet you came anyway. You said something about your trust fund? Is your family rich?"

"I don't have anything to do with my father's company or his money. He owns an investment brokerage firm in the Northern Quadrant," Aiden shrugged. "I work in a coffee shop so I can have money of my own. My grandmother set up a trust for me just before she died. She was an amazing woman and always stood up for me against my father," Aiden smiled and Ranger found himself stroking his mate's fingers. "Anyhow, she died about ten years ago; according to the will, I was to receive my trust fund on my twenty-fifth birthday."

"That was three months ago."

"You must have memorized my application form." Ranger shrugged. He had a lot of skills; his mate would find them out in time. "But yeah, it was three months ago," Aiden continued. "I asked my father about it of course, but he told me it would take time to release the money; something about audits and accounting procedures. I couldn't afford to leave my father's house until I got money of my own. I have a little in savings, but every time I suggested getting a studio apartment or something, Father would get angry and claim I wouldn't be safe."

"Is your father Alpha of your pack?"

Aiden nodded. Just then the waiter reappeared carrying their appetizers. Ranger let go of Aiden's hand so the table was clear for their plates, but even then, he almost ended up wearing his. "I'm so sorry," the waiter dabbed a cloth on his jacket.

"Scat," Ranger said with a growl and a flick of his fingers. The young wolf scampered.

"No wonder you don't go out much," Aiden chuckled and Ranger shook his head. Picking up his fork, he quickly scoffed down his food, unwilling to talk while they were eating. As soon as Aiden cleared his plate, Ranger stacked them and put them on a nearby empty table.

"Now, you were telling me your father is Alpha. I presume you're not in line to take that position?"

"Hardly," Aiden laughed. "I have six older brothers, all built like brick outhouses, and just as dumb. I think that's why my grandmother left me the money. So I'd have some independence and wouldn't have to be living with my father for the rest of my life. I only got the job in the coffee shop because the owners were new and lion shifters. They didn't care when my father threatened them. They owned the building so there wasn't anything my father could threaten them with."

"Your father sounds like a bit of a tyrant." Among other things. Ranger had a feeling he and his father-in-law were not going to get along.

"He's okay," Aiden said surprisingly. "My mom," he dropped his head. "My mom died giving birth to me. I don't think my father could ever forgive me for that. Once I got older, it was hard for him because I look so much like her. My brothers all take after him."

Ranger patted his hand, grateful when the waiter made another appearance. But as he methodically cut and chewed his food without tasting it, he couldn't shake the feeling his father-in-law deliberately set his youngest son up for murder-by-council. He just wasn't sure what he could do about it.

Chapter Six

Gods, I want this...I so want this...but what if...I should tell him...No, he'll think I'm silly... Aiden's thoughts were a scattered mess as Ranger unlocked the door of his private room. The rest of the dinner was uneventful apart from the waiter giving Ranger his phone number with the bill, and a couple of fearful mutters from other patrons as they left. Ranger ignored the number and the comments, so Aiden did too. In the car, Ranger seemed relaxed although still not overly talkative. Aiden's wolf was happy wallowing in Ranger's scent that seemed to increase the longer they were together. The wolf side of him wanted the claiming. A powerful assassin like Ranger made the perfect protector and the wolf was well prepared to belly up.

The human side of Aiden was a bundle of nervous anticipation. Ranger didn't seem like the affectionate type. He was probably a fuck 'em up against the wall type of lover. *I suppose I could handle that.* Ranger got the door unlocked and stepped back to let Aiden enter first. Guess he didn't have to worry about danger. They were on a council base and anyone stupid enough to be waiting in an assassin's room was asking for trouble.

The room was basic. A couple of chairs, a table that served as desk and dining, a door that presumably led to the bathroom and a large bed…with someone already in it. Aiden growled before he could stop himself. "You've got a lover and yet you brought me back here? What the hell were you thinking?"

"What?" Ranger roared and strode over to the bed. Aiden didn't know whether to leave or go, but his wolf was all for staying. Ranger was theirs. No question about it.

"I told you Cam was the one who did casual flings," Ranger snarled, throwing back the blankets and picking up a slender looking twink by the neck. "I asked you for mating forms for fuck's sake. Can't you take a hint?"

"I...er...you smelled real good," the twink gasped quickly. "I thought you were talking about me and you. My dad said you know your mates by their scent. I've been waiting for hours for you to claim me."

"How old are you?" Aiden asked, intrigued. He knew the twink wasn't his mate, so he wasn't worried Ranger might be.

"I'll be nineteen in six weeks."

Eighteen. Aiden shook his head. "I bet a wienner smells pretty good too," he said.

"I don't get horny over hot dogs." The twink's face was bright red.

"No, but a stiff breeze will tent your pants; when you're wearing any. How did you get in here?" Aiden went over and stood by Ranger's side, slipping his hand into Ranger's back pocket.

"My boss has a master key to all the rooms on the base," the young wolf was turning sulky now.

"You might want to return it before you get caught," Aiden warned. "Ranger, hon, let him go," his free hand stroked over Ranger's arm. "This pup can't help it if your power's a natural aphrodisiac. Look at the waiter in the restaurant. His pants were a mess by the time we finished eating."

"Now you can see why I don't go out much," Ranger dropped the twink on the floor and half-turned, pulling Aiden tight to his body. "The more I growl, the more they want to get their hands on me. Makes my skin crawl most of the time."

Aiden's heart melted. "You're touching me," he reminded the assassin gently; his body supremely conscious of the hard hands on his hips.

"I've wanted to do that all evening," Ranger's voice dropped. "And now I'm going to kiss you."

Aiden closed his eyes and tilted his head. He didn't have long to wait. Ranger's touch was gentle at first; almost cautious, but as Ranger inhaled, a deep growl rumbled in the bigger man's chest and it was like a switch was flicked. Aiden's lips were pressed, licked and nibbled as Ranger seemed determined to devour him. His hand still firmly in Ranger's pocket gave Aiden pulling power and he used it as leverage to get as close to his mate as possible.

"Fuck, you taste delicious. I knew you would," Ranger mumbled against his lips. "So good. So right. All MINE."

"Yours," Aiden agreed faintly. *This is what being with a mate is like? I'll never get anything else done.* But in that moment, Aiden didn't want to be anywhere else; couldn't think of anything else except the power of the arms crushing him tight, the lips burning his own and the heady scent of his mate making his knees weak.

And the boner pressing against his stomach; Aiden was definitely focused on that. His was threatening the seams in his pants and he begrudged the clothes that separated them. *Could I? Should I?* Fortunately, Ranger seemed to be of the same mind.

"Bed," he said roughly. "Bed or I swear by all that's holy I'll have you up against this wall."

Aiden looked across at the bed. Unbelievably the twink was still sitting on it; a hand wrapped around his cock and a rapt look on his face. "The wall might be our only option, although I don't want that guy seeing your naked butt," he said.

"You didn't have the decency to leave? This is my mate!" Ranger spun around with Aiden still in his arms. Aiden's feet got tangled with each other and he fell. *At least I made the bed,* but it seemed Ranger was hell bent on getting the interloper off it. "Horny fucking bastard," Ranger roared as he grabbed the twink's ankle, and holding him tight, dragged him off the tangled sheets and stalked towards the door.

"Not my face," the twink yelled as Ranger threw him into the hallway.

"Gods almighty," Ranger said and then he saw the clothes in Aiden's hands. "Oh no, he's not finding an excuse to come back in here." He snatched the clothes from Aiden's hands and threw then out into the hallway too, slamming the door hard.

"Those were my clothes," Aiden said with a chuckle. "But it's okay," he said when Ranger's panicked face turned back towards the door. "My wallet's here, I'll grab the rest later. How about you get rid of your clothes and join me?"

"The bed's going to stink of that pup," Ranger grumbled as he tugged his shirt over his head without bothering with the buttons, and slipped the button holding his pants.

"I won't let it bother me if you don't," Aiden promised as Ranger shoved his pants down his thighs and kicked off his boots. Gravity did the rest and Aiden quickly licked his lips. He didn't want his drool showing. He barely had a chance to register a v-shaped torso, one-half decorated with stunning black tattoos; tanned skin, and thick thighs, when Ranger was on him. The sensation of skin on skin was enough to make him gasp out loud.

*****

Slowly, must go slowly, Ranger kept telling himself but for once, his wolf was stronger than his will and was pushing him forward; wanting to stake his claim. Yes, sex for him in the past was something quick, relieving an itch; and about as pleasurable as taking a piss after a night's drinking. But this; a man only got a claiming once and even if Ranger wasn't worried about specifics, he would not let his new mate down.

His wolf let him know Aiden was inexperienced; which would explain the nervousness. Ranger would just have to make Aiden so wild with lust any pain on entry would be minimal. *Preparation...must...cock...every man likes his cock touched, right?* And it seemed that would be a yes because as soon as Ranger wrapped his hand around Aiden's sizeable length, his fingers were coated in come.

"I'm so sorry," Aiden said in between gulping air. "It's been...I've never...Oh wow."

Ranger wanted to laugh. "It's not a bad thing. In fact, it's hellishly flattering." Aiden's face was the color of cooked lobster and Ranger found kissing the man was a good way of diverting him from his embarrassment. Unfortunately, kissing Aiden had side effects.

Ranger was humping the blankets. Aiden's skin was silky smooth, warm to touch and Ranger's cock was begging to plunder what would be an exceptionally tight hole. He felt a growl erupting from his chest at the thought of being the only one...

"Lube. I've got to get the lube," he muttered against Aiden's lips. The look on Aiden's face was definitely from the "what the hell are you waiting for" category and Ranger leaned across the bed; fumbling in his drawer. *Yes!* He might not have sex very often, but rubbing one off was as much a part of Ranger's morning and nightly routine as brushing his teeth.

"Did you want me to turn over?" Aiden asked and Ranger was about to say "yes" but he bit his lip instead, shaking his head.

"It would be more comfortable for you that way," he said, "but I think our wolves would be happier if we could see each other." The relief on

Aiden's face forced Ranger's misgivings away.

This is a claiming; it's important, he told himself as he fumbled with the lube cap; hearing it ping on the floor when he forced it. Aiden's body resisted him at first. The boy was happily holding his legs up; nodded his approval at the pillow Ranger used to prop up his hips but when Ranger circled that sweet little hole, Aiden's body shut up shop like a clam.

"Squeeze tight," Ranger said. Aiden's eyes widened, but then crossed as he did what Ranger asked. *Cam said twenty to thirty seconds, one...two...ha. More like ten in a shifter.* Making a mental note to tell Cam later, Ranger kept his single finger pressure on Aiden's ass until it opened for him like magic. *Don't pump, don't pump; let him get used to it.* Aiden moaned and twitched his hips. His cock was hard on his abdomen, jerking as though seeking friction.

Should I? Could I? I should. Ranger flicked his hair over one shoulder and bent his head as a second finger joined the first. His first taste of cock seared a permanent brand on his memory. Oh yeah, he'd be doing this again. Ranger sucked gently, not giving Aiden the friction he craved, but keeping his cock alert. Two fingers became three, then four and finally, it was Aiden who yelled, "Get on with it."

Finally. Ranger never worked so hard for a fuck in his life; but as his cock slid home, and it was home; he brushed the curls from Aiden's face he knew in that instant that fuck was the wrong word to use. *This is what making love is like,* he thought and something of his thoughts must have shown on his face because Aiden beamed. His face was red, his forehead was gleaming with sweat that trapped the curls, but in that moment Ranger swore he saw heaven and he loved it.

"You okay?" He asked softly.

Aiden nodded. "I just...." Aiden's hips came up a bit and Ranger got the message. Thanking the Fates for super slick lube, Ranger moved; gently at first but Aiden wasn't having any of that. "More. Gods. Please." Ranger caved to the demands of his wolf. His body fell forward and he braced himself on his elbows on the either side of Aiden's face. His hips powered his cock into Aiden's body; his abs becoming slick from Aiden's precome.

Ranger grunted as Aiden looped his arms around his neck. *Oh yeah.*

Slick skin.

Hot hole.

Tight testicles.

Oh damn.

Not going to last!

Ranger felt his wolf surge alongside his orgasm. His teeth dropped and he growled; Aiden immediately presented his neck. *Glory days.*

One last hard thrust and Ranger lost it; his teeth sliced through Aiden's neck; his cock pulsed hard enough he thought he'd pass out and as bliss raced through his body, he felt Aiden tense and then a sharp nip on his neck as he was claimed in return. Teeth still embedded in Aiden's neck, Ranger managed a grin. It seemed his little mate had more strength than he'd bargained for. Being mated to an assassin, that wasn't a bad thing.

Chapter Seven

"Rise and shine; I've brought you breakfast." Cam's cheery voice was not what Aiden wanted to wake up to; especially, when he was having a lovely dream. Ranger, the hunky assassin had swept him into his arms and shown him how wonderful sex could be. He opened his eyes as the covers moved. *Wow. Not a dream,* he thought as Ranger growled.

"Newly mated; don't you know the rules? You do not disturb."

"We have things to discuss; most importantly, is your blushing mate going to finish the training. Because if he's not, there're more forms to fill out."

"I told you yesterday, I have to finish the course." Aiden made sure he was covered; his eyes pleading with Ranger who didn't look pleased.

"Get dressed and we'll discuss it over breakfast," Ranger said gently.

Aiden looked around the room. "You threw my clothes out in the hallway last night."

"Shit. So I did," Ranger scowled as Cam laughed. "Wait here."

I wasn't going anywhere. Aiden might not know a lot about mates, but he wasn't silly enough to get out of bed naked with Cam in the room. Ranger didn't seem to have that problem; flinging the covers back and striding over to a small dresser.

"You guys should probably shower too," Cam waved a hand in front of his face. Ranger just growled again, flinging a tee shirt and a pair of what looked like bike pants in Aiden's direction.

"It's all I have that will fit you. Get them on and we'll eat first," Ranger said, pulling on a pair of sweats.

Aiden looked down at the dried come on his stomach and felt more of it on the backs of his thighs. Ranger's shirt and bike shorts were too big and made him look like a homeless urchin. Still, at least he was covered. He gingerly got out of bed; his face heating further as Cam laughed at his discomfort. His ass didn't hurt, which was a positive point, but the dried come was itchy.

"As a top, it's your job to see to it you clean your mate off when you've finished dirtying him up," Cam told Ranger who flicked him off.

"How're the trainees?" Ranger filled a plate and set it in front of Aiden, before getting one for himself.

"Wondering how to turn your surprise announcement to their advantage," Cam said swallowing around a large mouthful. Half of his plate was empty already and Aiden sped up. He hadn't realized how hungry he was.

"Half of them think Aiden was a plant; sent in to report back secretly," Cam continued. "The other half think getting on Aiden's good side will help make things easier for them."

"How do you know all that?" Aiden's forked wavered just in front of his mouth.

"I hear things." Cam grinned at him.

"Cam is my research guy; back up and everything else you want to think of," Ranger said. "We were born in the same pack; we've been together for life."

"But we've never fucked. We're both tops," Cam said pointedly to Aiden who blushed even more and concentrated on his food. He was annoyed the blond picked up his jealous thoughts even though he was sure they didn't show on his face.

"You'll get used to him," Ranger said. "He thinks he's funny."

"I am," Cam protested and both men laughed, leaving Aiden to eat.

Ranger, to his credit, didn't say anything else about him training until Aiden's plate was empty and he was cradling a half-empty cup of coffee.

"You said last night that your father won't release your inheritance unless you complete this week's training. Is that right?"

"Yes," Aiden nodded. "I didn't even know what this place was for. Father just said he was sending me to camp. I had to complete the week and when I did, he'd release my funds."

"This is money he should have received three months ago. It would give him complete independence," Ranger said to Cam. Cam's eyebrows lifted.

"Something smells fishy," Cam said.

"It's worse," Ranger said. "My mate's signature is not on his intake form. Only his father's, the alpha of the pack Aiden grew up in."

"That could make completion difficult," Cam said and he was all serious now. "I don't know how the hell you got through the intake, but without that signature, neither Ranger nor I can sign you off as finished. You shouldn't even be here."

"Can't I sign it now?" Aiden panicked. All he wanted was what was left to him. He didn't know why his father insisted on him doing the training course. He probably should've asked. But he counted on his father's agreement to give him the strength to do whatever was asked.

"We'll back date it," Cam said, nodding in agreement. "Anyone asks, we found out about the form the day he arrived and got him to sign it before he did anything. No one will know, and no one's likely to question either you or me, Ranger."

"Except the person who rubber-stamped his application in the first place," Ranger said grimly. "This has got Dominic written all over it."

"The guy you were talking with yesterday?" Aiden asked. "I've never met him before. I'd have recognized the voice."

"But he is the ruling council member for the Northern states," Ranger said. "There's an excellent chance he knows your father."

Aiden slumped, his eyes swimming with tears he was frantically trying to hide. He was tired. Tired of being picked on by his brothers; tired of his father's indifference. And now, if Ranger was to be believed his sire roped the council in on their scheme. Whatever that was.

"Hey, you're going to get your money," Ranger's warmth circled him like a blanket as he found himself pulled into his mate's arms. "You don't need it; I have more than enough for both of us," he grinned as Aiden lifted his head and glared. "But this is important to you; it was left to you by your grandmother and while we don't know why your dad's doing this," but we will, was the look he gave to Cam, "you will get your completion certificate."

"But father knows I didn't sign it before I came here," Aiden felt his hopes rise.

"I'll explain the situation when we see him." Ranger's voice was so firm, so strong, and Aiden melted into his mate's embrace. His wolf told him he could trust Ranger, so he would.

"I've got some things I want to research on the computer. Can you take this morning's training by yourself, Ranger? We're doing time trials over the same obstacle course," Cam pushed his chair from the table.

Ranger nodded and simply held Aiden until Cam had gone. Then Aiden felt his chin being tilted. "I know you're a man of honor and finishing this course is important to you."

Aiden managed a small nod. He felt a wave of lust hit him and saw an answering need in Ranger's eyes.

"I'm not going to take that away from you," Ranger continued after a long moment. "However, as your mate, I can't let you become one of the council's statistics either."

Yeah, I'm not too keen on that side of things. "What do you want me to do?"

Ranger grinned. "Stick by me. We're mates. It'll be expected. I'll train you as hard as everyone else, so no one can claim favoritism or special privilege, but I will make sure you're safe."

Ranger's lips were heading for his, and as Aiden closed his eyes, he wondered briefly, how much of this training business was going to hurt. He didn't want to end up pissed off at his mate.

Chapter Eight

"He's going to hate you, you know," Cam whispered as Ranger watched the trainees slogging through the rain and mud. Aiden was unrecognizable. His face and clothes were covered in grime, his back half-bent by the hundred-pound pack weighing him down.

"I did tell him he didn't have to do this." Ranger shook his head. Three days claimed and all Aiden had the energy for when he was finished for the day was sleep. To be honest, Ranger was miffed. Impressed, because Aiden was keeping up with the other men in the team; they were all bigger and stronger. But miffed that his mate wouldn't take advantage of his position and stay by his side where Ranger wanted him.

The episode over breakfast that morning was a classic example. Ranger and Cam had devised a training program that worked on increasing stamina in the mornings and then hand to hand combat skills in the afternoon. It'd been raining hard all night and Ranger knew the course would be slippery and muddy. He couldn't lighten Aiden's pack or he'd be accused of favoritism. So, he'd suggested, very reasonably he thought given he was as horny as hell that Aiden give up on the run completely. Turned out having a mate meant it wasn't acceptable to give his cock a solo workout morning and night like he was used to and Aiden seemed determined to crawl out of bed the moment the alarm went off.

Aiden didn't like his suggestion. In fact, Ranger remembered terms like "overbearing" being used along with a snarled, "You just want me to fail so I'll be dependent on you for life." While it would be helpful in their future life for Aiden to have some independence, Ranger was still smarting about his mate's attitude. This was not what he'd been told would happen as far as mates were concerned.

"I did get some intel on Aiden's father if you're interested," Cam said as Ranger cringed when Aiden slid in a patch of mud and landed on his ass. It infuriated him that no one would help him but the last time Ranger offered to help, Aiden pushed him out of the way.

"Go on," he said, his fists clenched as he watched Aiden struggle. The weight of his pack and the slipperiness of the ground weren't making it easy. A couple of men laughed as they ran past and that upset Ranger even more.

"Seems Alpha Chalmers has made some bad investments," Cam said before going, "Ouch, that has to hurt," as Aiden made it partially up before slipping and falling right on his tailbone.

"What do you mean bad investments?" Ranger turned to his friend. He couldn't watch. His wolf was ready to jump out and kill the next person that laughed at his mate and he wanted nothing more than to drag Aiden back to his room and fuck him in the shower before tying him to the bed.

"He's in debt up to his eyeballs," Cam confided. "I also found out there's a five million dollar insurance policy on your young mate. Taken out two weeks ago; payable to the father in the event of death by any cause."

"Five million dollars?" When Ranger heard Aiden had an inheritance he was thinking a hundred thousand at most. "Were you able to find out how much Aiden's trust fund is?"

"He didn't tell you?" Cam raised his eyebrow. Ranger frowned and waited. He wasn't about to tell his friend his mating was having a few difficulties and that he and Aiden barely had time to chat about anything. Cam huffed. "I checked into it because my first thought when I found out about Alpha Chalmers was that he was dipping into Aiden's money. But as of last night, the trust was intact; roughly two hundred twenty-two million dollars and change. It seems

Grandma Chalmers was a very astute business lady and while the will left the company to her son, the house and the bulk of her money went to Aiden."

"That's why his father didn't want him to move out," Ranger growled.

"Oh, his father and brothers should have moved out years ago. The house became Aiden's when he turned twenty-one. The money is tied up until his twenty-fifth birthday, but there was a substantial lump sum for house maintenance left to cover his costs until he received his money. I can't find any sign Aiden had use of that, but his father and brothers have."

"He was working in a coffee shop, trying to save money for a studio apartment before he came here."

"Then there's a good chance your mate doesn't know the contents of the will. I can get you a copy if you and your mate want to meet me at the Swamp later."

"Yeah, I owe you a drink or three," Ranger sighed. He saw Kendall, the little twink who almost derailed his mating coming towards him. It wasn't going to be good news if the man was braving the weather. "Looks like duty calls. Can you give my mate a hand? If I do it, he's likely to bite it off."

"Trouble in paradise?"

"Let's just say, I'll be glad when this fucking week's over." Ranger glared at Kendall. "What now?"

"Councilman Dominic's compliments; he's waiting in your office."

"Watch him," Cam said as he headed over to a bedraggled Aiden. Ranger wasn't sure if he meant Kendall or Dominic.

*****

Aiden smacked the mud in disgust. He was sick of being wet; sick of being tired. He was ready to punch the next man who laughed at him and he was heartsick over the way he spoke to Ranger that morning. His wolf was pining; his guts had been churning all morning and he was miserable. For an alpha wolf, Ranger had taken his stubbornness surprisingly well. He hadn't complained about Aiden being too tired for sex. He woke up every morning with the big man's arms around him and a woody poking his butt. He hadn't said a word about the fact Aiden was normally snoring by the time it took for his mate to strip out of his clothes at night. He'd done his best not to show favoritism in front of the others, and all told, Aiden figured Ranger deserved a medal for the way he was handling things.

While you just come across as a spoiled child. Aiden slapped the mud again and was rewarded with a splatter right beneath his eye. He wiped it off in disgust.

"You know, if you wanted a facial, you only had to ask." Cam loomed over him, holding out his hand. Aiden took it, struggled to his feet and then looked around for Ranger.

"Dominic wanted to see him," Cam said, hefting the big pack off Aiden's shoulders as if it was nothing. "He wanted to help you, but he's got the idea you would bite his hand off or something." He started jogging towards the dorm rooms and Aiden automatically followed.

"Yeah, I've been a prick to him," Aiden confessed. "It's not his fault. He hasn't done anything wrong. It's just, I've waited for my inheritance for so long; to be finally free of my father for good, and I just can't throw it all away because of Ranger's alphaness."

"Alphaness," Cam laughed. "Good word. Or you could try assassinitis. He gets that every time he goes out on a job. You'll learn to handle it over time."

"I know he's getting impatient with me and I can't blame him. My inheritance probably isn't that much anyway, but my grandmother told me it would be enough for me to live comfortably and it's the last thing I'll ever have of hers, you know. I want to know she'd be proud of me."

"You do know a quick trip to the lawyer would have given you your inheritance anyway, don't you? You don't have to put yourself through this." Cam indicated his mud-splattered clothes and drenched hair.

"The only lawyer I know is a friend of my father's and he wouldn't help me," Aiden said glumly. "I don't have a copy of the will or anything except a letter from my grandmother telling me she was leaving me some money. I don't think that's going to help."

Cam steered him away from the main dorms and towards Ranger's apartment. When they got to the door, he smiled. "Why don't you shower; I'll send up some lunch and you can spend the rest of the afternoon catching up on your sleep."

Aiden opened his mouth to protest and Cam shook his finger. "No. I'm giving you an order. I know it's important for you to do this training week by yourself. But you're only doing it to prove something to your father. One of the keys to being an adult is learning to accept help when you need it. You are mated to this country's top assassin. While Ranger might not be good for much more than looking pretty and tracking down his prey, I, on the other hand, have a lot of skills that will be helpful in your situation. Clean up. Eat. Rest. Don't disobey me. Tonight, when Ranger asks you to accompany him to the Swamp for a drink put a smile on your face; ease that delicious booty into your tightest pants and say yes. We've got you covered."

Still confused, Aiden let himself into Ranger's room, closing the door behind him. He was immediately conscious of his soggy, muddy state. Stripping off his clothes, he left them in a heap by the door. When whoever brought him lunch, he'd ask for a trash bag. He didn't think the stains would ever come out. Naked, he padded across to the bathroom and got the shower running. Moments later he was moaning as the mud and grass fell out of his hair and into the drain below. It felt like forever since he'd taken a shower during the day.

Could it be that simple? Aiden wondered as he shampooed his hair. *Could Cam sort out my inheritance without me having to kill myself or wreck my mating?* Sexually inexperienced he might be, but even Aiden knew that the urge to have sex with a mate was almost constant. The only reason he hadn't been feeling it was because he'd pushed himself harder than anyone else on the team.

Staying under the shower until his skin was wrinkled and the water was running cold, Aiden wasted no time drying himself off and climbing into bed. The sheets smelled of Ranger and he moaned. *I've been a damned fool.* His last thought as he fell asleep was that he would be a lot better mate.

Chapter Nine

Ranger clamped his teeth together, stopping his snarl as he strode into his office. Dominic was leaning over his desk, peering at some papers. "Did you lose something?" He snapped, his lips curling as Dominic scuttled away from the desk. Sitting down, Ranger quickly glanced over the papers Kendall left there. Requisition orders; nothing to worry about then.

"I have another job for you," Dominic said, sitting down and smoothing his pants with his palms.

"Cam and I are here for two more days and then I told you, I'm taking the rest of my vacation."

"This is just a little job. Hardly worth using your skills for it," Dominic pulled a piece of paper out of his jacket. "It's just you're here already, so I thought why not?"

Ranger frowned and leaned his elbows on his desk. "There's been a kill order put out on someone in this camp? Who?" The only people currently in the camp were the trainees and support staff.

"Not a council kill order, exactly," Dominic looked down at his piece of paper. "More of a personal favor for a friend; you'll get your usual rate and you won't even have to leave the camp. I'm sure you can make it look like an accident."

Ranger's heart dropped and he had a sinking feeling in his stomach. "I presume you're talking about one of my trainees. What's he done to upset your *friend?*"

"Nothing you need to worry about. One more kill's not going to bother you. I just need you to make sure this particular person doesn't leave the camp on Friday."

Leaning back in his chair, Ranger kept his face bland and his eyes sharp. Dominic was nervous. Not only could Ranger smell it but the way the man kept fiddling with his shirt cuffs was a dead giveaway.

"Who do I need to kill?" If Ranger didn't take the job, then someone else would and with his mate in camp, he didn't want any of the other assassins around.

"Aiden Chalmers." Dominic leaned forward and put his paper on the desk. The bile rose in Ranger's throat as he stared at the picture of his mate. "Make it quick," Dominic continued. "My friend doesn't need an example made of this man. He just needs him out of the way. A carefully staged accident will ensure any insurance claims will go through with no problems. You know how it is. It's not as though you haven't done something similar before a dozen times. And this camp is renowned for its hard training methods. No one is going to bat an eyelid if this man doesn't make it home. I'm surprised he's not dead already." Dominic sneered at the picture and Ranger's wolf rose in defense.

"I'll take care of it," he said firmly.

"It'll give you more money to spend on your vacation," Dominic flashed a quick smile but was clearly rattled by the lack of expression on Ranger's face. "No need to let me know when it's done. My friend will be notified through the usual channels. I'll speak to you when you get back from vacation." Opening the door, Dominic slipped out. It was clear he wanted as few people as possible to know about his visit.

You will see me a lot sooner than that, Ranger promised as he picked up Aiden's picture. His mate's clear blue eyes shone back at him and he traced the blond curls and those full lips. A picture of innocence. How the hell someone as lovely as Aiden crawled out from the cesspit of his father's pack was anyone's guess. But Ranger was determined to protect his mate to his dying breath. If that meant wiping out the Chalmers family line and a couple of corrupt councilmembers while he was at it; Ranger didn't care. It's what the council had trained him for.

Thank the Fates my mating forms are locked in a drawer, he thought as he hurried out of the office to find Cam. He wouldn't be handing them to Dominic just yet. In fact, he'd rather bypass Dominic altogether until he and his best friend had devised a plan.

*****

Aiden dressed with care. Feeling a lot better after a nap and food, he was waiting in bed naked when Ranger came in. He hoped awake and naked were all the cues Ranger needed to join him. But something was clearly bothering his mate and after a peck on the cheek, Ranger said he needed to shower and that they were going into town. Aiden was puzzled by that. The gossip among the trainees indicated the Swamp was a bar on the base.

No worries, he thought. He was actually going to spend time with his mate and he wasn't covered in mud, slop or bruises. Remembering their first dinner date and the fantastic night he and Ranger shared when dinner was done, Aiden made a mental note not to drink too much. He was desperate to feel his mate's cock pounding his ass and his wolf longed for their connection. *Tonight,* he promised himself.

"You look really good," Ranger said and Aiden turned, hoping Ranger would be naked. Unfortunately, he was already dressed. His long black hair hung down his back like a satin sheet; barely seen against the black shirt and pants Ranger wore. The only shiny things were his mate's boot and belt buckles, and the gleam in his mate's eyes. Aiden flushed under the heat and fiddled with the button on his shirt.

"We could stay in," he offered shyly. What he knew about seduction wouldn't cover a pinhead.

"I'd like nothing more," Ranger said coming over and kissing the top of Aiden's head. "However, Cam and I have things to discuss with you. That's why we're going to town; Fewer eavesdroppers."

Aiden was disappointed, but remembering the mud from earlier; the bruises he'd sustained over the past four days and the constant taunts from his fellow trainees, he figured if Cam found a way for him to get his inheritance without doing any more training, he'd say thank you and be grateful. The one clear thing he decided during his afternoon alone was that Ranger should and would be his sole focus from now on. Once he had his money; he'd pack his meager belongings and flip his father and brothers off as he walked out of the door of the mansion that had sucked his soul dry.

Chapter Ten

The place Ranger chose for dinner was in a hotel. He'd booked a private room and the hostess wasted no time showing them through. Cam was already sitting at a table set for three.

"Hi guys," Cam always seemed to be smiling. "This place has the best lobster. I've ordered two portions already."

"You can run the training in the morning then," Ranger said as he held out a chair for Aiden. Aiden blushed. He wasn't used to someone being so courteous and he picked up the napkin, placing it on his lap as Ranger slid into the seat beside him.

"I've already ordered for us," Ranger said quietly, "but the menu is beside you. If there's anything else you want, you just have to ask."

"I'm sure whatever you ordered will be fine." Aiden didn't have a lot of experience with fancy meals. He was more of a steak and fries fan. But he made appreciative noises when the food was put silently in front of him and didn't have any problems clearing his plates. It was tasty, even if he had no idea what the entrees were called. Cam and Ranger chatted about the trainees; reminisced about a couple of places they'd been and it wasn't until the coffee had been served and the doors closed, giving the three men their privacy, that Cam picked up a briefcase from under the table.

"Okay, Aiden. I told you at lunchtime that I would see what I could do about your situation. Ranger gave me some other news this afternoon which might impact a few things. But he can tell you that in a minute. Firstly, I wanted to give you a copy of your trust records. This is your balance with the bank as of lunchtime today."

Cam handed Aiden a piece of paper. A bank statement. His

money was lodged with the Northern States bank not far from where he lived. He used to walk past the building every day on his way to work at the coffee shop. But the location or name of the bank wasn't what had Aiden reaching for his glass of water. "This can't be right. You must have mixed this up with my father's account." His eyes couldn't seem to make sense of all the digits in the account balance column. There were eleven of them; nine of them on the left-hand side of the decimal point. He put his glass back down and counted to make sure. The account balance was in the hundreds of millions of dollars. Two hundred twenty-two million dollars to be exact.

"It is all yours," Cam said gently. "I checked with a lawyer friend of mine from the Northern States. He drove down to the bank personally, flashed his credentials and claimed he was acting on your behalf." Aiden stared at him; his eyes wide. "As of two pm this afternoon, the entire balance of the account has been transferred to your lawyer's escrow account in another bank. He is waiting on your instructions." Cam handed Aiden a business card. "You'll find he's a nice guy and totally trustworthy."

"You...you've dealt with him before?" Aiden knew his voice was shaky. He couldn't get over the staggering amount of money his grandmother left him. She said he'd be comfortable for life. He could buy a freaking island with the balance he was looking at.

"The lawyer's my brother and he knows you're Ranger's mate."

"Newton knows better than to mess with me," Ranger said with a chuckle. Aiden felt a hot hand on his knee. "You'll be fine; you won't get ripped off. Newton was top of his class at University and he's been working in investment and tax law since he left school. He's clever and extremely loyal to his clients."

Aiden wasn't thinking about his newly-acquired lawyer. He shook the bank statement in his hand. "This...Can I access this money now? It's mine?"

"Yes," Cam said firmly. "We got a copy of your birth certificate from the council records. Ranger signed the authority as your mate to hire Newton to deal with the matter. We felt it best to move it from the bank seeing as your father is a shareholder there, but yep. It's yours. No one can take it away. We would have asked you first, but you look adorable when you're sleeping."

"I don't know what to say," Aiden was still in shock. Cam and Ranger had solved all his problems while he was taking a nap. "I, there's no way I can thank you guys. You've...I thought I'd have to battle my father for months about this and that's when I was hoping for something like twenty grand. This is unbelievable."

"It's done now," Ranger said, stroking Aiden's knee. "No matter what happens, there is no way your father can get his hands on your inheritance, especially now you're mated."

"I am, aren't I." Aiden's cheeks ached as his mouth stretched into a grin. "I feel like I've won the lottery."

Ranger and Cam shared a look and the smile dropped off Aiden's face like a stone. "What is it? There's a catch isn't there? What is it? Have I inherited a five hundred million dollar debt as part of my inheritance too?"

"Nothing like that, but there is more," Ranger said. "Cam, give him the will."

Cam handed Aiden more documents stapled together. It was from the law firm his father used. Aiden's eyes filled as he read "Last Will and Testament: Alpha Dorothy Chalmers." He looked up at Cam and Ranger. "She was the best alpha our pack ever had," he said softly.

Ranger nodded. Aiden went back to reading the contents. The company went to his father. He already knew that. His six brothers each received a hundred thousand dollars on their twenty-first birthdays. *That didn't last them long,* he thought, remembering how his brothers were always sucking up to Father for more allowance.

For my grandson Aiden Chalmers. He sniffed and blinked, close to tears. Then his eyes widened as he kept reading. He read the paragraph again and then a third time just to make sure his eyes weren't playing tricks on him.

"The house has been mine since I was twenty-one? I've been living in my own house for the past four years?"

Cam nodded. "From what Newton could find in his quick search, the house was transferred into your name, in accordance with the will, two days after your twenty-first birthday. Your father took control of the maintenance account at the same time and has been helping himself to it ever since."

"I could never work it out," Aiden seethed. "Never work out why he kept stopping me from working; wouldn't let me leave home. I begged him; pleaded with him to let me live my own life. The only life mission my brothers ever had was to make mine hell and they succeeded. But you're telling me, the only reason they kept me around is because they had no right to live in the house without me?"

"As you can see, the will was very specific about that. None of your family members could share your home unless you were living there, too." Cam shook his head. "Your grandmother was trying to protect you from being manipulated."

"I need to go," Aiden turned to Ranger. "I need to have this out with my father. He didn't tell me. Nobody told me. I have to speak to him."

"Aiden, my mate, my one and only," Ranger's hand on his cheek was so gentle and his eyes looked pained. "There's one more thing you should know before flying off. Dominic came to see me this afternoon to give me an assassin job."

"So you can't come with me?" Aiden's mind was in turmoil. All he could think about was speaking to his father. He'd prefer it if Ranger came with him, but he'd make the trip alone if he had to. "Should I wait? Will it take long? What do you want me to do?"

"This isn't like one of my normal jobs," Ranger seemed to be picking his words carefully and Aiden held back his growl of frustration. "Dominic ordered the kill as a favor to a friend in the Northern States. There's no easy way to say this. My next contract is you."

Aiden's mouth dropped open. Ranger's finger edged it shut. He swallowed and then swallowed again. "I need a drink," he said roughly when he could get his mouth to work. "Stuff the glass. I need a bottle of the strongest drink known to shifters. If anyone ever had an excuse for getting drunk it's got to be me today."

Ranger and Cam shared another look and then Cam got up and went to the door, speaking to someone on the other side of it. Aiden took Ranger's hand from his face and held onto it tight, staring at the table. *When will this freaking roller coaster ever stop?*

Chapter Eleven

Ranger smiled in the darkness as Aiden rolled, snuffled and then started to snore. His mate was a lightweight when it came to drinking…and a flirt. Ranger was glad he'd booked a suite at the hotel. He wasn't sure he or the car would've made it back to base with Aiden trying to strip him at every opportunity. As much as Ranger longed to sink into his mate's delicious ass, he wouldn't do that while Aiden was so plastered. He succumbed to a sloppy blowjob; Aiden was too cute and sexy to refuse but by the time he'd returned the favor, Aiden was asleep.

Tucked up, nothing but his tousled curls on display, Ranger longed to slide in next to him. But he was waiting and as he heard the quick click of the door lock, he knew his wait was over. "Hello Marcus," he said quietly, his nose catching the familiar scent. "Is Shadow with you? Oh yes, there he is. Evening Shadow."

A side light clicked on and Shadow tilted his head. Marcus was staring at the bed, sniffing the air. "It's not like you to fuck a mark before you kill him, Ranger," Marcus said. "Sounds like that's more Cam's thing than yours."

"Aiden is a special case," Ranger said quietly.

"Must be," Shadow leaned towards the bed. "Has he got super powers or something? Because there's nothing I could see on his file that warranted two assassins on the job."

"Dominic send you?" Ranger asked although he already knew the answer.

"Yeah, he called yesterday. Said it was a rush job," Marcus said, keeping his voice low. "We went out to the base but a randy twink said you were out for the evening and you'd taken Aiden with you. It wasn't hard to track you down. Your car is parked right out front."

"Intentionally." Ranger knew Dominic was up to no good.

"I don't understand why we were called in," Shadow threw up his hands. "You've got the mark. You've clearly got the job covered. So, what the fuck?"

"Maybe the guy's a virgin and Ranger's giving him an assassin special before he offs him. The deadline isn't until Friday." Marcus laughed. Ranger didn't. Marcus stopped and looked at Ranger in confusion. "You're protecting him?"

"Do you remember a certain case, oh three years back now?" Ranger pulled out his pack of cigarettes and lit one. Non-smoking rules were the least of his worries. "Let me think. It was a full council job. A petty thief stole something important to the council and me and you Marcus, were sent to get him. Do you remember what happened?"

"Yeah," Shadow laughed and threw his arms around Marcus's neck. "He caught me. One sniff and my pants were ripped off, ass up and this guy's cock was in me so fast I couldn't catch a breath. It wasn't until his teeth were in my neck, I realized what had happened. Best excuse for turning legit I'd ever found."

"Aiden's yours." It wasn't a question but Ranger inclined his head at Marcus. "Well, shit. Guess this is one job we don't have to finish, little one. Let's head off and get a room of our own."

"Actually," Ranger stood and indicated the two chairs by the side of the bed. "You're going to sit your asses down and tell me everything Dominic said to convince you to take this job. It is not a request." He pulled aside the edge of his long coat, showing his knives and Marcus frowned. He sat down, pulling Shadow onto his lap.

"There's no need to be like this, Ranger. We trained together. I know you can beat me, but there's no need. As I said, me and Shadow will disappear. I don't want any trouble with you. If anything, I owe you a dozen favors."

"That's good because I'm about to call them in." Ranger smiled and proceeded to tell his friends Aiden's situation, his words punctuated by his mate's heavy snores.

*****

"Mother of god; whatever that shit was, don't ever let me touch it again," Aiden rolled over, one hand clutching his head, the other searching for his mate. The sheets beside him were cool to the touch. Prying his eyes open Aiden stared at the blank space before scanning the room. Ranger was sitting at the table with two other people.

"Er...hello." Aiden checked under the sheets. He was naked. Crap. He needed the bathroom and food in that order.

"You're finally awake," Ranger grinned at him, coming over to the bed with a cup of coffee. "Drink this and you'll feel a lot better."

"*I need to pee*," Aiden mouthed to his mate. He pointed under the sheets. Ranger's eyebrow raised and then he nodded.

"I'll get you a robe and you can say hello to our guests." Ranger went over to the bathroom door and pulled one of the complementary robes from a hook on the back of it.

I already said hello and I need to pee, like now, Aiden thought frantically. He grabbed the robe Ranger handed to him; quickly slipped it on and scrambled out of bed.

"Hello again," he said quickly to the two men at the table, tilting his head slightly. The bigger man at the table was a wolf shifter and Aiden's eyes widened slightly at the star tattoo under the man's left eye. "I'm Aiden Chalmers; if you'll excuse me I have an urgent appointment with a porcelain bowl."

He dashed through to the bathroom and slammed the door shut behind him. Unfortunately, the sound of his peeing didn't hide the laughter coming from the others in the bedroom.

Damn rude, Aiden thought as he shook himself off and went to wash his hands and face. *What's Ranger thinking, letting people into our room when I was sleeping?* He scowled at his reflection. His eyes looked tired, there was a definite throbbing in his head and his curls were all over the place. *Tough. They will just have to accept me as I am.* He tightened the tie around his robe and holding his head high, went back into the other room, sitting at the table. There was enough food there to feed an army, but Aiden focused on the cup of coffee Ranger put in front of him.

"I'm Marcus," the bigger man held out his hand. "This is my mate, Shadow. He's a cat shifter."

Aiden put down his mug and shook the hands offered. "Nice to meet you," he said, picking up his cup as soon as his hands were free. "I presume you're friends of Ranger's."

"Actually, we were looking for you. But Ranger said we couldn't kill you so we decided to stay for a late breakfast instead." Shadow buttered some toast. "Ranger and Marcus trained together."

Aiden was glad he'd just swallowed. He put his mug down with shaky hands. "You came to kill me?" He looked at Ranger, his eyes about to pop out of his head. "How many more people have a contract out on me?"

"As far as we know, just me and your mate," Marcus said. "But then Levi wouldn't take the job and Sean's out of the country. You're having brunch with the only two assassins on the case."

"Peachy." Aiden longed to sit on Ranger's lap; or better yet, pull his mate back to bed and pull the covers over his head. Unfortunately, he didn't know how his mate felt about PDA.

"I was worried Dominic would do something like this," Ranger said, filling his mug again. "Because Cam wasn't able to confirm if any rank-and-file soldiers would be after you too, Marcus and Shadow agreed to help protect you. Cam will be here shortly and we'll all go and visit your father and get this matter dealt with."

"I still can't believe my father would put out a hit on me," Aiden glared at the table cloth. "It seems a bit extreme. I mean, I know the inheritance was a sizable sum of money, but he has plenty of money of his own. I'd sell him the damned house for a dollar if he wanted it."

"Sold." Shadow reached into his pocket and pulled out a dollar, slamming it on the table.

"How about you see how you feel about the place once it's empty before you go giving it away?" Ranger picked up the dollar and handed it back to Shadow, who laughed and put it back in his pocket.

"What about the trainees," Aiden asked. "There's still today and tomorrow to go. Won't Dominic think it's suspicious if you and Cam aren't there?"

Marcus and Ranger laughed. "That won't be a problem," Marcus said between chuckles. "Your mate called in another favor. The official assassin trainer, Tron is going to handle those little wannabes for two days. And all internet access and phones have been cut until the end of the training to stop anyone complaining to the council or their daddies. If Dominic does turn up, he'll shit himself."

"Dominic is terrified of Tron and Tron's agreed to hold the councilman if he does go creeping around the base," Ranger explained. "Tron's always had authority issues."

"Dominic was the one who ordered the facial tattoos," Shadow said, stabbing his knife into the butter. "Claimed rogues needed to know it was a council hit as they breathed their last. Never fucking cared what it would do to an assassin's social life."

Marcus took the knife out of Shadow's hand and handed him a freshly buttered piece of toast. "We're the strongest of our kind," he said gently and Aiden got the impression the two men had had similar conversations before. "That little tattoo used to get me a lot of sexy attention before you came along and stole my heart."

"Yeah," Aiden remembered Kendall and the waiter at their first date. "Men seem to fall all over assassins. Women too, I imagine."

"Wouldn't know. Don't care." Marcus shuddered. Shadow laughed.

Aiden felt a warm hand on his neck and turned to Ranger with a smile. "You know mated wolves can't be unfaithful, don't you?" Ranger asked quietly.

"I do now." Aiden leaned into Ranger's hand. He really wished the other two would leave so he could show his assassin how much he cared about him and how thankful he was for all that was being done for him. He mentally cursed the fact he was too drunk to do much the night before.

But a sharp knock on the door reminded him they had more important things to do and any thoughts of sex fled his mind as he realized he was going to have to confront his father. He wasn't good with confrontation. He always felt like he was twelve when he stood in front of his father, and while there were a lot of things that needed to be said between them, he wasn't sure he was going to like the answers his father might have. Maybe Ranger's presence would be enough to shock his father into telling the truth. But somehow, Aiden already knew the man who raised him wasn't going to admit to anything anytime soon. Not without a damned good incentive and definitely not in front of witnesses if that admission could get him into trouble. *I wonder if he really wants the house that badly.*

Chapter Twelve

"Please tell me you'll think twice before letting your father keep this house," Ranger said quietly as Aiden's home came into view. Hidden behind a huge gate, the driveway was long and there were no other houses in sight. The house itself was two story; with a dark brick façade broken by twenty-two latticed windows, Ranger could see. The front of the house had six white columns adding further relief from the dark exterior and five attic windows perched on the roof.

There was a large sweeping driveway that ran in front of the house and disappeared into some trees; Ranger assumed it led to garages. Big. Private. Quiet. Easy to protect. He turned off the engine and looked around. Yep, he could see himself living here.

"It's not a fun place with my brothers living here," Aiden whispered, glancing at the door.

"They won't be living here," Ranger replied. "Come on. Let's get this done. Cam and the others are giving us ten minutes then they're coming in. They are scouting the perimeter in the meantime, waiting for our other resources to get into place."

Ranger knew he should offer some sort of comfort to his anxious mate. Aiden was trying hard to hide his nerves, but his hands were shaking and his bottom lip was being abused by his teeth. Unfortunately, they were on a time schedule. "Have you got a dining room table?" He asked as they walked silently up the steps.

"Yeah. Big formal thing. Seats about forty people. That'll be the first thing I want out of here," Aiden shuddered.

"Not until I've fucked you on it," Ranger promised, pleased the gasp stopped Aiden abusing his lip. He stood to one side and let Aiden open the door, curious to see how his mate would be greeted in his family home.

"Aiden, what the hell are you doing here?" A gruff older voice yelled. "You're supposed to be at that camp until tomorrow. Don't bother me with your excuses. You ran away, didn't you? It got too tough for you. Fucking typical. Well, don't say I didn't warn you. If you can't show you're mature enough to handle one little camp for one short week, I'm damned sure you're not mature enough to handle your inheritance."

"Actually, Father, I thought I'd come home because I have exciting news I wanted to share. I thought it was better than trying to explain on the phone." Aiden reached his hand back and Ranger took it, following his mate into a large living area. There was only one man in the room. Older, Alpha, and dressed in a bright purple smoking jacket of all things. "You won't have to worry about me being mature enough to handle my inheritance anymore. I found my true mate and I've been claimed. Ranger, meet Alpha Chalmers of the Northern States. Father, meet Ranger. As you can see from the tattoo on his face, he's an assassin. In fact, he's the best one they have and he's my true mate."

Chalmers's mouth dropped open, his eyes bulged and he made as if to get out of his chair. "You brought an assassin into my house?"

"Your house?" Ranger shook his head and Chalmers sat back on the chair, his tanned face going white.

"Yes, why didn't you tell me the house was mine?" Aiden sat down in another chair facing his father. Ranger stayed standing. His ears were letting him know they weren't alone in the house. "Ranger's friend. He's amazing. He can find any information on anything. Well, when Ranger claimed me, he wanted me to stop training and I explained why I couldn't because of what you'd told me about the inheritance. But he said he'd handle it for me." Aiden threw Ranger a huge smile and Ranger's eyes narrowed slightly. There had to be a reason for his mate acting like a child.

"Handle it for you?" Of course, the older Chalmers would seize on that little nugget of information. "Your inheritance is in a trust. It doesn't need handling. I just need to sign the papers and the money's all yours."

"You don't need to worry about it," Aiden leaned back in his chair, the picture of ease to most people. Ranger wasn't fooled and he moved closer. "It's already been taken care of. Ranger's friend arranged for a lawyer to hold my money for me and as soon as Ranger and I can sort out joint accounts, it'll be transferred there."

"You took the money out of the bank? Without talking to me?" Chalmers jumped to his feet, his fists clenched and a red hue started creeping up his neck.

"I don't know what there is to talk about, Father." Aiden studied his nails. "The money's mine and while I know you have shares in the Northern States bank, that doesn't mean I had to keep my money there. It's not as though we're close."

"That money represents almost seventy-five percent of the assets in that bank. You can't just take it out!"

Aiden shrugged. "It didn't belong to the bank."

Ranger's ears caught the sound of someone moving down the staircase in the corner of the room; someone trying to be quiet and failing. He slipped his hands into his pockets.

"I really don't know why you're upset, Father," Aiden said, his voice calm. "It was my money, left to me by my grandmother. Maybe if you'd given it to me when I asked, or better yet, let me move out of the house when I asked, then I wouldn't have felt the need to move my funds elsewhere."

"You did this because I wanted to keep you SAFE?" Chalmers's yells were obviously trying to mask the sound of footsteps.

Ranger kept one eye on Chalmers and one on the stairs. One shadow; and then the second one appeared. Faster than a blink Ranger threw two of his stars at the offending shadows. Yells, thumps and the clatter of rifles falling on the marble rang around the room.

"Fucking hell, I've been hit."

"I'm bleeding."

Two men stumbled into view, both clutching an arm. From the family resemblance to the older Chalmers, Ranger guessed these were two of Aiden's brothers. "Don't you know better than to pull a rifle on an assassin?" He growled.

One of the men pouted, examining his arm. It was only a small gash.

"Aiden was the target, not you. I thought you were supposed to have killed him already. Can't do your job? Did he roll over and present his ass, begging you to spare his life?"

"Shut up, Bevan!" Chalmers said quickly, but it was too late. Ranger snarled; the sound low and menacing. *Don't open your mouth because I swear, just one more word….*

"Hey, it's okay," the other Chalmers clone whacked Bevan on the chest. "Remember that council dude said he had a backup. I guess you're dead meat, after all, little brother."

And that's the word. His leather coat swirling away from his legs, Ranger covered the distance in seconds. One long swipe and both men fell to the floor, silent.

"Are they dead?" Aiden's eyes were wide and Ranger hurriedly pocketed his knife and went and put his hand on his mate's shoulder.

"It was quick, which is more than they deserved."

"You killed my sons in my own house." Chalmers fell on his chair, his face in his hands.

Ranger heard Aiden inhale sharply. "It's not your house. Haven't you been listening to me, Father? I already know this house is mine and you and my brothers had no right to be living here."

Chalmers lifted his head quickly. "You can't know that…how…no…he promised."

"Who promised what?" Cam sauntered into the room, Newton beside him. "Did someone promise you Aiden wouldn't see a copy of his grandmother's will? When council law specifically states all last wishes have to be held in public record?"

"I…er…no…er…who the hell are you?"

"You don't have to worry who I am," Cam smiled and inclined his head towards Newton. "It's this guy you should really be concerned about. Meet Newton Lock, Aiden's lawyer."

"Mr. Chalmers?" Newton said, resting his briefcase on the back of Aiden's chair and opening it. "I have here a court order for you and your six…" He looked over to where two bodies were slumped on the floor. "Sorry…make that four sons, to vacate these premises immediately. A council lawyer will be appointed to oversee the packing of your personal effects. All chattel and household items belong to my client, as per the terms of the late Alpha Chalmers's will."

"You can't throw me out of my home. I've got nowhere to go." Ranger's hand on Aiden's shoulder tightened. But Aiden didn't have a chance to say anything because Newton got in first.

"Accommodations won't be a problem. These gentlemen are here to escort you to the council base, where you will be held on charges of attempting to procure a murder, attempted murder, fraud, embezzlement and failing to adhere to council estate laws." Newton clapped and four men entered the room dressed in council uniforms. But they weren't council soldiers. Ranger recognized Brian and Gerald and two other men from the training course. He managed a tight smile.

"I haven't done anything," Chalmers wailed, totally ignoring the bodies of his sons and the rifles on the floor. "I just need to talk to my son and this whole mess can get sorted out."

"Which son," Shadow called out cheerfully as he and Marcus came in; each tugging two bodies tied together with ropes. "Four more counts of attempted murder to add to your charge sheet, Newton. We caught these two," he slapped the men he was holding around the head, "trying to get a clear shot through the window."

"And these two were sabotaging the car. We'll need new brakes before we go anywhere," Marcus said, slapping his two before dropping them in a heap and sticking his foot on them.

"There're plenty of cars in the garage," Aiden said. "I understand they're mine, too?" He asked Newton.

Newton nodded. "Everything in the house, grounds and yes, that includes the garages."

"There's a lovely black Lamborghini in the garage," Aiden's lips were trembling as he stared at Ranger. "It'd suit you perfectly."

"You'll have plenty of time to show me everything once we clear the mess out." Ranger caressed the side of Aiden's face, showing him without words how proud he was of how his mate was holding up so far.

"Aiden, we need to talk. None of this was meant to happen. Everything's just got a little out of hand." The older Chalmers looked broken and Ranger assumed that he'd spend the rest of his life regretting he'd been caught. Ranger didn't care if he never saw the man again, but his mate probably would. But Aiden surprised him yet again.

"I've tried to talk to you my whole life," Aiden said firmly, facing his father who was now being held between Brian and Gerald. "It's you who never had the time for me. If you'd been honest, shared the details of grandma's will; allowed me to move out, which was all I ever wanted, and not thrown up so many obstacles to my having access to my inheritance, all of this could have been avoided."

He reached for Ranger's hand. "Instead you sent me to a training camp where the death rate is known to be high. You arranged with a corrupt councilmember for me to be killed for no reason at all, except you didn't have the legal means to control me anymore. Well, you know what Father? You did me one hell of a favor. Because if it wasn't for you, I wouldn't have met the man I love with all my heart. I wouldn't have made good and honest friends and I wouldn't be standing here in this fancy house, over two hundred million dollars richer. Think about that when you're sitting in your cell. Your fate is your doing, not mine."

"You're worth over two hundred million dollars?" Brian yelled. "Shit. Can I be your friend?"

Aiden laughed and turned to Ranger, his eyes as clear, honest and bright as they'd ever been. "You had that chance when we were in camp. You'll have to take that up with my mate."

Ranger gave into the temptation he'd had since he'd entered Aiden's home and pulled him out of the chair, holding him tight against his chest. His mate didn't need to watch his father and brothers being carted away, or the mess being cleaned from the floor. Fortunately, he knew the perfect distraction.

Chapter Thirteen

Aiden needed Ranger like he needed air. His dad, his brothers, the house and his inheritance; his brain was overloaded and he did not want to think. He needed to feel, needed something to shut his brain down.

Ranger's arms were heaven around his back; lips perfect against his. There was noise, a lot of noise around them. Aiden heard his name called, yelled and cursed at but he didn't care. He moaned against Ranger's mouth and thrust his cock against a solid thigh.

"Your room?" Ranger pulled back from his lips long enough to ask. His eyes blazed and there was a wealth of promise behind the lump in his pants.

Aiden gasped, swallowed and managed to say, "Up the stairs, third on the right."

Thank the Fates for a take charge mate, Aiden thought as Ranger lifted him off his feet. Aiden's legs wrapped instinctively around Ranger's hips, hidden from view by the long leather coat his mate still wore. He sucked and nibbled the long arc of throat exposed to him as Ranger made his way purposefully across the room, up the stairs and into the room Aiden had lived in his whole life. It was still as he left it, although Aiden caught the scents of his father and at least four of his brothers lingering in the air. *Fuck them, they can't hurt me anymore.*

Ranger didn't waste time checking out the decor. Four strides and they were on the bed, Ranger's weight pinning him down in delicious fashion. "Need you," the big man muttered before he started tearing at Aiden's clothes; the actions showing just a hint of the speed and power Aiden witnessed earlier. In his arms, Aiden relaxed and the more he fell under Ranger's spell the hornier he felt.

"Quick this time," he begged as Ranger's mouth teased his nipple. "I want to feel you in me."

Ranger's body was tightly controlled, his movements quick and efficient. A lube packet was dug out of Ranger's pocket and Aiden pushed back the moment he felt fingers on his ass. There were muffled clunks as Ranger moved; *weapons?* Aiden wondered, but then they were drowned out by the sound of Ranger's zipper being opened. *That's the best sound in the universe.* He hummed, his body impatient and as Ranger turned him on his side, he went eagerly although he missed his mate's weight.

"One leg up." Ranger lifted Aiden's top leg and pushed it away from him, exposing Aiden's ass in a way that would have him blushing if it wasn't for the hunger eating his soul. It was more than getting his rocks off, although his cock appreciated it when Ranger grabbed it like a handle and plunged into his body.

"Yes," Aiden grasped. "Full."

"That what you wanted, babe?" Ranger's tongue and lips were teasing his neck, the top of his shoulders. Aiden tilted his neck giving his mate more access.

"Just move, please move."

"I have to take this slow." Ranger's voice caressed his ear. "It feels like forever since we've done this."

"I need to stop thinking." Aiden bit his lip but the confession tumbled out anyway.

"I'll stop you thinking."

Ranger made good on his promise. His big body moved with grace and precision. His cock teased and tormented Aiden until he was a babbling mess. His hands scrabbled around on the covers, Ranger's hands the only thing keeping him grounded. Everywhere his mate touched, Aiden's body tingled. Ranger's mouth scorched his skin as a trail of marks was left over his neck and shoulders and all the while, Ranger held him close. Intermittent endearments peppered Aiden's ear. He wanted to respond but his brain wouldn't work. All that came out of his mouth was gasps, moans and a plea for Ranger to never stop.

It was his cock that signaled the end, or rather his balls. Ranger's hand kept up a steady rhythm, enough to keep Aiden on the edge without pushing him over. But a finger brushing over his balls with every downstroke was hardening his balls at an alarming rate. All too soon… yep, Aiden couldn't fight it. He gave a long groan as his cock spurted, making sure his ass tightened around Ranger.

"Oh damn, your smell." Ranger folded over Aiden's side, his body gently shuddering as he reached his climax. Through the haze of afterglow, Aiden became aware of Ranger's buttons digging into his side. He slid his legs back against his mate. "You still have your boots on," he said with a chuckle.

/~/~/~/~/

Ranger was well aware he was still dressed, and while it seemed like a good idea before the act, he wished he was naked now. Aiden was warm and relaxed in his arms and Ranger wanted to wallow in it. Unfortunately, he figured they probably had to talk before they headed downstairs. There were a few ramifications of the day's events, Aiden probably hadn't thought of.

He carefully eased from Aiden's body. "Stay here. I'll be back in a second."

"Bathroom's over there." Aiden waved in the general direction of the corner of the room as he snuggled into the covers. Ranger found the bathroom. His mate's room had all the mod-cons and the multi-headed shower gave him pause. *Later,* he told himself firmly. He stripped out of his clothes and washed himself off before grabbing a washcloth and going back into the bedroom. Aiden moved in response to his hands, movements he kept deliberately gentle.

"Throw it on the floor," Aiden muttered and Ranger was worried his mate would fall asleep. He couldn't let that happen. Not just yet.

Dropping the washcloth on the floor, Ranger climbed onto the bed and dragged up the spare blanket, covering them both. "Come on you," he teased, "it's not nap time yet."

"I feel safe with you and I feel like I could sleep for a week." Aiden rolled over so they were facing each other. Ranger was struck by the trust in his mate's eyes.

"I'd never hurt you," He promised softly, "but I'm not going to ignore the fact I killed two of your brothers today. I can't apologize for doing what any decent mate would do, but I'd like to know how you feel about it now."

"Nothing," Aiden said quickly, but then he thought for a moment. "Actually, that's not true. I'm grieving the fact my brothers will never be who I'd hope they'd be. Does that make sense?"

Ranger nodded. "I don't have any family to share, unfortunately. Assassins have to be loners before they're even considered for the program."

"Is it hard, your job?"

Considering his answer, Ranger pulled Aiden close. As always, his mate melted in his arms. "I don't take a life lightly," he said at last, his fingers finding pleasure running over Aiden's skin. "There are a lot of evil paranormals out there, just like humans. If killing someone saves an innocent, or a persecuted group then no, it's not hard at all."

"Dominic asked you to kill me and you took the job." Aiden wasn't questioning him, Ranger understood that. He was trying to understand a lifestyle he had no experience with. That thought warmed Ranger's heart.

"I did that for two reasons," he explained. "Firstly, I didn't know it was you who was the target when I said yes. I just didn't want another assassin in the camp with you there. Secondly, all four of us, the current assassins, we all get given jobs we don't like. Many years ago, we all got together and decided that there were some things the council didn't need to know about."

"You mean you don't kill everyone you're told to?" Aiden's eyes were wide, but his hands were relaxed as they looped around Ranger's neck.

"Marcus and Shadow wouldn't have killed you, even if I hadn't been there," Ranger said. "They would have done their homework; just like Cam and I do on every job we're given. When they found out you were an innocent and your death was purely for financial gain, they would've hidden you until they could solve your problem for you."

"Sort of like underground superheroes." Aiden smiled. "I like it."

"The council puts their pants on the same way we do and sometimes they make mistakes, or believe false information," Ranger explained. "Dominic was usually more circumspect about things, but this time he blatantly said the job was a favor for a friend. It's not like him to be so careless."

"He probably owes my father money," Aiden said glumly. "A lot of people do."

"I hope it was a lot of money then because Dominic's already in jail. He's lost his career, his home, and everything because of this. The rest of the council is furious at the way he abused his position.

Attempting to kill the next Alpha of the Northern States is frowned on by everyone."

"I can…hang on a minute?" Aiden's bright blue eyes were sharp. "I'm not the Alpha Heir. My brother, Bevan is. He's the eldest. I'm the youngest, remember?"

"You didn't read the rest of your grandmother's will, did you?" Ranger watched as Aiden slowly shook his head. "Your father was never Alpha. He was Alpha Regent. He was supposed to be holding the job until you came of age."

"Which, for wolves, is twenty-five." Understanding dawned on Aiden's face. "But how, why? I was only fifteen when my grandmother died. I was nothing like my brothers in terms of strength and size. How could she leave the position to me?"

"She knew your heart," Ranger said gravely cupping Aiden's cheeks. "She wasn't the strongest either, but she was a good woman and she wanted someone to care for her pack, not profit from it and use it for their own gain."

"Why didn't someone tell me? The pack enforcers would've known. They always know the succession before anyone else." Aiden's eyes were wet and Ranger wondered what type of relationship he had with the enforcers. To be honest, Ranger was surprised he hadn't been met with more force when they'd arrived. He didn't have a pack affiliation and his tattoo marked him as a danger to anyone who saw him.

"How many of the current enforcers used to work for your grandmother?"

Aiden was quiet for a moment and then he frowned. "None of them," he said, brushing his eyes quickly. "The current ones were all picked by my father about five years ago. I always thought it was strange they were never allowed in the house. This place was built to house all ten enforcers, plus the ruling family. It was always full of pack members when my grandmother was alive."

"Your father was making sure no one could tell you he was only regent and not actually Alpha. I bet none of the original enforcers live in this pack anymore."

"That's a shame. They were good people." Aiden's voice went quiet. "What will happen to him? My father, I mean? I know they weren't council soldiers that took him unless the team have received a promotion since yesterday."

Ranger bit his lip against the *who cares* comment that teased it. Aiden was holding himself together really well considering the bombshells he'd dealt with in the past week. Ranger reminded himself it was part of a mate's job to be supportive. "We decided to use the trainees because using regular council soldiers would've alerted Dominic we were onto him. There'll be a proper council hearing to assess the charges. I imagine they'll be more concerned about the fact that your father abused his position as regent, didn't file your grandmother's will the way he was meant to, and probably embezzled funds from the bank. Because you're still breathing, he can only be tried for attempting to procure murder, although they may make a big deal about it, given you are the Alpha now."

"I'm n...he's not getting out of jail, is he?" A whole slew of emotions flashed across Aiden's face including fear and horror. Ranger shook his head.

"I'm the Alpha of the Northern States."

Ranger nodded.

"I haven't got a freaking clue what to do." Aiden buried his head in Ranger's neck.

"Don't worry about it, babe," Ranger said softly. "That's why I'm glad you have a huge house. Cam will help, Marcus and Shadow and the other assassins will as well when I can contact them. Newton will be by your side, as will I. You will get through this."

Aiden's curls tickled Ranger's face as he shook his head. Then his face popped up. "Won't you have to go to work?"

"I'm thinking now might be a good time to retire," Ranger smiled. "Marcus has already spoken to me about your security and the ideas he has for this place. Shadow reckons an infant with a screwdriver could break into this place."

"Well, we don't want that, do we?" Aiden tilted his head up for a kiss, which Ranger was happy to give him.

"I do love you," he said gravely, making sure a now relaxed Aiden was meeting his eyes. "It might not be a great declaration like yours downstairs earlier, but I mean it from the bottom of my heart and I always will."

Aiden's cheeks flamed but his gaze never wavered. "I love you too. And you'll help me, won't you, deal with all the mess my father has probably left behind."

"I'll be right by your side."

"That'll freak out the stuffed shirts who run the bank," Aiden laughed. Ranger joined in, determined to see to it that his lovely mate with a heart of gold got to laugh every single day of their lives together. He could make it a rule as Alpha Mate.

Freaking hell, I'm Alpha Mate. Now it was Ranger's turn to want to hide under the blankets, although he made sure Aiden didn't have a clue how much the thought horrified him. *Having to deal with people all day. UGH.*

Chapter Fourteen

A week later.

Aiden coughed and covered his mouth to hide his smirk. Don Jenkins, CEO of Northern States Bank was more than a little perturbed when he turned up, complete with lawyer, two men wearing assassin marks and the affable Cam who still managed to look intimidating. Marcus made Shadow stay at the house; apparently, the bank might be too tempting for the reformed cat burglar. But Aiden was glad of his new friends as he took the offered seat. Newton sat beside him, but the rest of his entourage stayed standing.

"Aiden..." Jenkins broke off when Ranger growled at him and started again. "Alpha Chalmers, I wasn't aware you were coming in this morning. Was there a problem with your account?"

"Why don't you tell me?" Aiden never liked Jenkins. The man was a beta wolf who acted like an alpha every chance he got. "As I understand it, you and my father are the sole shareholders in this bank. The council has now ruled that all my father's assets be transferred to me. However, after investigating my father's accounts it appears both you and he took substantial fees from my inheritance account on a monthly basis. I want to know why."

"Oh, yes, well, that's common banking practice," Jenkins cast a nervous look at the other men in the room. "You will find all banks charge an administration fee when handling such a large sum of money. The money is paid out of the monthly interest accrued and doesn't impact the capital balance in any way."

"Is it customary for *all* of the interest in an invested account be then withdrawn as bank fees?" Aiden held out his hand and Newton handed him some documents. "From what I can see here, my grandmother entrusted you with two hundred twenty-two million dollars, is that right?"

Jenkins gulped. "That's correct."

"And the interest rate for any investment is customarily five percent per annum as deemed by council laws. Is that correct, or does this bank not follow council laws?"

"Oh no, we follow the council laws to the letter." Jenkins was quick to assure him.

"But not in accordance with fees it would seem." Aiden scanned the papers in his hands although he already knew what was in them. Ranger, Cam, and Newton rehearsed this scenario with him a dozen times before they would let him face the bank manager. They wouldn't interfere unless Jenkins did something stupid.

"According to my calculations, five percent of the capital balance is eleven million dollars per year.

Council regulations state that banks can only take half a percent per annum of that money in fees. Or in this case fifty-five thousand dollars a year. Correct?" Aiden looked up.

"Er, yes, but…"

"So by my calculations, and please let me know if I am wrong in any way. My account is short one hundred nine million, four hundred fifty thousand dollars without including compound interest over the ten years you've held my account. Where is it?"

Jenkins went green. Aiden didn't think it was possible for anyone, except maybe a demon to go that color, but Jenkins's skin took on a green tinge. "We had a lot of expenses," he said quickly. "There were losses made in investments that had to be covered. Your father didn't want any pack members to lose any of their investments due to changes in the financial markets."

"But the money hasn't gone to pack members," Aiden glanced at his papers again. "Seventy-five percent of it went to my father's accounts, and twenty-five percent of it was paid each year into your private bank account. How is that benefiting the pack or its members?"

"Your father and I both contribute substantially to charities in this territory." Jenkins was trying to take the upper hand, something Ranger warned Aiden he would do.

"The one's on this list?" Aiden held out his hand again and Newton was ready with another piece of paper. "I've visited these charitable organizations as you call them over the past few days. Imagine my surprise when I went to visit the orphanage that according to publicly held records you give a hundred thousand dollars a year to and found out it was a brothel; and not a well-run one at that. Or the LGBTQ homeless shelter, something vital in this region;

turns out that it's a bar. As for the soup kitchen; tell me, does Doris Brown make soup in her own kitchen? Where does she distribute it because I'm sure I can drum up more support for her efforts? She must make a lot of soup to the tune of seventy-five thousand dollars a year."

Jenkins's face went puce at the mention of his mistress's name. "Now you listen here, you little upstart," he yelled. "Just because you're wearing a fancy suit and bring a posse of bodyguards does not mean you know what goes on in this territory. Your father and I…."

"Bled this territory dry," Aiden interrupted angrily. "I've spoken to the council. There isn't any help for wolves or other paranormals in the Northern States. This bank hands out loans and mortgages at twenty percent interest and then when people can't afford to pay, they are stripped of their belongings and kicked out. Each state territory has a bank that is supposed to help the people in the surrounding territory, not rob them of everything they own."

"You don't know what you're talking about. Your father and I run this territory and no one complains."

"Because you have any complainers killed, bankrupted or run out of town. I've had enough." Aiden stood up. "Cam, the box please." Cam threw Aiden a cardboard box which Aiden slammed down on the desk. "Pack your things, Jenkins. You're out."

Jenkins stared at the box as if it was an alien object.

"You heard me, you're out. Fired. Caput. Gone. Clear your desk out and get out of my sight."

"You can't fire me; I'm the only shareholder left." Jenkins didn't touch the box.

"Wrong. It seems you don't listen very well. I own seventy-five percent of the bank. You *did* own twenty-five percent, but that along with my father's holdings have all been signed over by the council to me in repayment for the interest I am owed. I did my homework before I came here today, Jenkins; you should have done the same before you decided to rip me off."

"You won't get away with this. I challenge you for Alpha position of the Northern States," Jenkins snarled as he shifted and leaped up onto the desk, his lips curled upwards showing his teeth.

Aiden didn't move; didn't even blink. He knew Ranger was ready to intercept, but he refused to accept that unless it was a last resort. It'd shocked him to the core to find out he was the Alpha, but after a week of meeting people in town, he knew he could do a lot of good and he was determined no one was going to oust him from his place.

"That won't work either," he said, keeping his tone calm. "For one thing, even though I may look small, I'm still an alpha wolf and you'll never be more than a beta. Don't underestimate me. And even if you managed to get close to me and actually wound me, I'm mated. Fully claimed." He tugged his shirt collar aside showing the scar left by Ranger's teeth. "Under council law, you have to beat me and the Alpha Mate before you can take over this territory. Take a look around and guess which one of these men is my mate. Then make your move."

Jenkins growled again, the saliva dripping from his teeth, but he didn't move. Aiden could see the tension in his shoulder muscles and along the wolf's back, but it seemed Jenkins's desire for life was stronger than his need to be Alpha or his position at the bank. After a long minute, Jenkins laid his ears back and lay down on the desk, tilting his head.

"Wise move," Aiden said. "Now, as I have absolutely no wish to see you naked, I'll leave. You have thirty minutes. Thirty minutes to remove your personal effects from your office, home, and car. My lawyer, Newton Lock, will remain behind along with Cam and Marcus to ensure you don't touch or take anything that doesn't belong to you. When you have time to read these documents you will see all your buildings and other assets are to be sold, as ordered by the council, to help repay the damage you and my father have done to this territory. If I see you again, my mate will kill you." He slipped his hand around Ranger's arm. "He's the council's best assassin, you know."

Aiden found the strength to leave the bank building with his head held high. He made it to the car before his legs wobbled. "I don't know if I can do this," he whispered once Ranger slammed the door shut and they were alone.

Ranger sighed and then started the car, his free hand weighty on

Aiden's legs. "You can and you will. You were freaking brilliant in there. Now, hold on tight, I have something I want to show you," he said and Aiden relaxed in his seat as the throaty engine roared.

Chapter Fifteen

Ranger knew it was going to take a while for him to get used to his new role. Alpha Mate was a title he was going to have to live with. But letting Aiden do his job, to stand up to challenges such as the scene in Jenkins's office was a test of his control. Then there were the people. Lots of people. Ranger was a get the job done; hide away until the next one type of person. The tattoo on his face brought him a lot of attention he didn't want or need; although, to be fair, the Northern States pack seemed to accept him more readily than most. But Ranger knew that was Aiden's doing, not his. The people loved Aiden.

And so did he, which was why Ranger had turned his life upside down and why he was flogging the Lamborghini up the steep hills on the edge of the territory. Aiden could do with a break, and if he was honest with himself, Ranger wouldn't mind one either. Training at the council base camp had nothing on the meetings, queries, and duties Aiden had to contend with.

Seeing the small marker on the side of the road, Ranger turned off and followed the dirt track; the car's undercarriage protesting the whole time. Yes, he could have brought an SUV for the trip, but Ranger secretly loved driving the fancy car and figured a few potholes wouldn't hurt it. Parking in a small clearing, he dropped a quick kiss on Aiden's face before getting out. Everything was just as he'd asked it to be.

"You did this for me?" Aiden's smile couldn't have gotten any bigger. Ranger felt a blush hit the top of his cheeks but he managed a smile. *It's perfect. He'll love it. Don't sweat it.* "I thought you'd like to have lunch with me away from the curious hordes," he said, feeling self-conscious. "We haven't had much time for dating since we got together."

"I'm sorry," Aiden said, stepping close and slipping his arms around Ranger's waist. "But if I had to be on this roller coaster, I'm so glad you're on it with me. What made you think of all this?"

Ranger looked across at the small picnic table covered in a white cloth; the food already laid out and covered in cloches. "It was Cam's idea," he admitted knowing any lie would be smelled in an instant. "I don't know a lot about romantic gestures, but I wanted you to know how much I cared about you. That I see you as more than the heir to a fortune or an alpha. That I see you as the man I love and someone I want to spend all my time with."

"You show me you care every day," Aiden said softly. "The way you didn't yell at Jessie's five-year-old for spilling juice on your pants; or when you helped old Mrs. Forbes with her groceries and ate that brick she called a brownie without complaint. You talked to my enforcers, you haven't grumbled about sharing our house with so many people. Ranger, you've done a lot and for someone who's used to being alone…it means the world to me."

"I thought Jessie was going to have a heart attack, the way she looked at me, and as for Mrs. Forbes, I like her. She shouldn't be treated as a nuisance just because she's old."

"It was lovely spending the afternoon listening to tales of my grandmother, even if the coffee tasted gritty and the brownies almost broke my teeth." Aiden laughed and Ranger ticked that off his to-do list for the day.

Of course, it was on his list every day, but their relationship was still too new for him to assume he made Aiden happy. Aiden didn't have a formal pack meeting to announce his new position. He'd visited every house and business in the area, introducing himself and listening to every single concern.

It'd been a hectic time, and their personal moments together had been few and far between.

"Why don't you come and eat?" Ranger suggested, looking over at the table again. "Cam said we had the whole afternoon off and I'd like to just spend some quiet time with you."

"Kiss me first."

Ranger never needed asking twice. Aiden was sweet and good and innocent in a lot of ways. *Not as innocent as he was when I met him*, Ranger thought with a grin, but he kept their kissing light. He had a duty as a mate to ensure Aiden's wellbeing and the confrontation at the bank hadn't been easy on either of them. Pre-Aiden, Jenkins would have been dead for having the audacity to shift in front of him. *Can't be a killer all my life.*

Lunch was a huge success. Ranger might not have Cam's moves but he did pay attention. All Aiden's favorite foods had been included. Ranger did a mental shudder at the way Aiden poured ketchup over his fries but it wasn't as though he had to eat them.

"I needed this," Aiden said, pushing his plate away. "The view, the food, the amazing company." Aiden stroked Ranger's arm. Six months ago, he would've moved away. Now Ranger found he craved the connection. Which reminded him.

"I don't have a problem with you touching me when we're out, you know," he said, topping up Aiden's glass. Sweet mango juice. Ranger didn't want Aiden's pack mates seeing him drunk.

"I...er...I didn't want to presume," Aiden's head was down and Ranger tilted it up, smiling at the blush he knew would be there.

"We're a team, you and me, yeah?"

Aiden nodded.

"There's nothing I won't do for you."

"Same here." Aiden's cheeks were still red but the smile was back.

"There might be some who're jealous of our true mate bond, but that's their problem, not ours."

Aiden nodded.

"So, if you want a hug, or to hold my hand, you know sometimes I'd appreciate it."

"You mean, keep you safe from the horny lady wolves that look at the bulge in your pants and think pups." Aiden's grin grew wider.

"I don't have a problem with people knowing the true nature of our relationship," Ranger said, although Aiden had hit the nail on the head. His assassin tattoo had a lot to answer for in a species that put a lot of value on strength.

"Cam told me when we first met; you were used to being alone. I just didn't want to…."

"And you don't," Ranger interrupted quickly. "Has my life changed? It has. Has yours? Definitely. Are we in this together?"

"Indubitably."

"Then how about you trust me with everything?" Ranger stared into Aiden's eyes and knew his mate understood. In just a matter of weeks, Ranger had gone from being a tough assassin who preferred his own company to being Alpha Mate. Aiden's dreams of simply being allowed to move out from under his father's domain had come true, but the responsibilities he carried now were tough for young shoulders.

"I love you," Aiden said simply, "and yeah, I do trust you. With everything. You're my life."

The two men sat on the grass, watching out over their territory. There was a lot of talking, some quiet times and some pretty hot make-out sessions along the way.

But as they wandered back to the car, the picnic stuff cleared away, Ranger had one more question.

"You ever think about taking a vacation? We could let Cam and the others run this place for a while. Travel. See places."

"Leave your weapons behind for a change?"

Ranger shrugged; he wasn't going to promise the impossible. But as he drove the car back to their home, Aiden's excited chatter about the places he wanted to see filled him with warmth he'd never had. Thanking the Fates, he joined in the planning of their holiday, knowing that wherever life took him, Aiden would always be by his side.

Epilogue

"Here you go; something towards your study expenses." Cam handed the young blond a hundred.

"You don't have to. It's not as though we did anything, and I'm not a whore. All I did was sleep on your bed and you were on the couch," the blond protested although Cam could see the need in his eyes.

"I'm not suggesting you're a whore," Cam said quickly, giving the young man a hug. "It's just you told me about your studies and I know student life isn't easy."

"You sure?" The blond asked, but he was already slipping the bill into his pocket.

"Just remember our agreement," Cam warned.

"Never tell a living soul what went on tonight, unless someone gets pushy. Then tell them you're the best fuck I ever had." The blond wore a cheeky grin. "I don't mind finding out if that's true, you know."

"It ain't gonna happen, kid, now beat it. You have classes in a few hours. And yawn a couple of times for me."

The blond laughed and skipped out the door, full of the energy of youth after a good night's sleep. Cam closed the door with a sigh. He went over to his dresser and pulled out the picture he'd hidden there before his "date." It was a candid shot. Cam snapped it quickly during a job three years before and kept it ever since.

The man in the picture was proud, an arrogant look on his lean handsome face. His long black hair was similar to Ranger's although there were no highlights or colorful streaks in it. His body was hidden under the long leather trench coat the man was barely seen without, but Cam remembered every detail of their one night. The strength of the man's hands, the power of his thrusts and the unabashed pleasure that lined the man's face as he climaxed with a roar and a bite.

"Fucking bastard," Cam said sadly, stroking the features of the man's face in the picture. "Why couldn't I be good enough for you to stay?" he stared at the picture until a beep from his watch reminded him he had things to do. "I'll see you tonight," he said, popping the picture back in its hiding place. Checking his game face in the mirror, Cam smoothed back his hair, straightened his back, plastered on a smile and strode out of the room. With Ranger and Aiden on vacation, people were counting on him and he was proud of the fact he never let anyone down. Not even his mate.

About the Author

Lee Oliver is a pen name for author Lisa Oliver. Always known as "Tea-Lee" as a teenager because of her preference for that particular beverage, Lisa's tea drinking habit has remained, making her nickname the perfect pen name. Lee Oliver will be responsible for the short, easy to read, and hopefully enjoy, stories she's always wanted to write.

You can contact Lee/Lisa on Facebook at http://www.facebook.com/lisaoliverauthor, through her blog, http://www.supernaturalsmut.com or via email at yoursintuitively@gmail.com.

Other Books By Lisa Oliver

Cloverleah Pack

Book 1 – The Reluctant Wolf – Kane and Shawn

Book 2 – The Runaway Cat – Griff and Diablo

Book 3 – When No Doesn't Cut It – Damien and Scott

Book 3.5 – Never Go Back – Scott and Damien's Trip and a free story about Malacai and Elijah

Book 4 – Calming the Enforcer – Troy and Anton

Book 5 – Getting Close to the Omega – Dean and Matthew

Book 6 – Fae for All – Jax, Aelfric and Fafnir (M/M/M)

Book 7 – Watching Out for Fangs – Josh and Vadim

Book 8 – Tangling with Bears – Tobias, Luke and Kurt (M/M/M)

Book 9 – Angel in Black Leather – Adair and Vassago

Book 9.5 – Scenes from Cloverleah – four short stories featuring the men we've come to love

Book 10 – On The Brink – Teilo, Raff and Nereus (M/M/M)

Book 11 – (as yet untitled) – Marius and (shush, it's a secret) (Coming April 2017)

The God's Made Me Do It
(Cloverleah spin off series)

Get Over It – Madison and Sebastian's story (Coming February 2017)

Bound and Bonded Series

Book One – Don't Touch – Levi and Steel

Book Two – Topping the Dom – Pearson and Dante

Book Three – Total Submission – Kyle and Teric

Book Four – Fighting Fangs – Ace and Devin

Book Five – No Mate of Mine – Roger and Cam

Book Six – Undesirable Mate – Phillip and Kellen

Stockton Wolves Series

Book One – Get off My Case – Shane and Dimitri

Book Two – Copping a Lot of Sin – Ben, Sin and Gabriel (M/M/M)

Book Three – Mace's Awakening – Mace and Roan

Book Four – Don't Bite – Trent and Alexi

Book Five – (as yet untitled) – Captain Reynolds and Nico (Coming March 2017)

Alpha and Omega Series

Book One – The Biker's Omega – Marly and Trent

Book Two – Dance Around the Cop – Zander and Terry

Book 2.5 – Change of Plans - Q and Sully – short story, (Coming soon)

Book Three – The Artist and His Alpha – Caden and Sean

Book Four – Harder in Heels – Ronan and Asaph

The Portrain Pack and Coven

The Power of the Bite – Dax and Zane

The Fangs Between Us – Broz and Van – a Portrain Coven and Pack Prequel (coming soon).

Balance – Angels and Demons

The Viper's Heart – Raziel and Botis

Passion Punched King – Anael and Zagan – coming March 2017

Shifter's Uprising Series – in conjunction with Thomas J. Oliver

Book One – Uncaged – Carlin and Lucas

Book Two – Fly Free (Coming soon)

Made in the USA
Las Vegas, NV
13 July 2021